PRAISE FOR VIROZONE

"Lawlie is a strong female lead and would be very relatable to the intended YA audience. She is vivacious and tough, powering her way towards justice and not taking no for an answer" **Jess McFarlane, author of Widows Flame**

"Lawlie was a fun character to follow. She is determined, fierce, and does not waste time. Virozone is action-packed from cover to cover" **Liv Evans, author of The Underground**

"I definitely want to read the next book! Cole has left me hanging!" **KE Barden, author of The Gilded Mirror**

"The main protagonist, Lawlie, is packed with a punch! She is tough, determined, and refuses to let anyone hold her back - whether it be for her own safety or not." **Nikki Minty, author of Pastel Pink**

"What I loved most about Virozone is the character Lawlie. So often, the lead character in adventure stories is male, so Lawlie becomes a strong role model for young female readers" **Kristine Fitzgerald, author of The Ring of Toadstools.**

"Virozone is a great dystopian read for teens" **Maxx Victor, author of Cinder and Black.**

"I liked that the determination and strength of the protagonist was not a tacked-on attribute designed to adhere to the 'strong female' trope, but rather, an innate need of Lawlies, due to her lifestyle and the tragedy that befell her mother" **Michelle Ham, author of Just Deal With It.**

"Virozone has lots of interesting concepts of a dystopian world set in the future. It's definitely a worthy read for anyone with an interest in that middle grade level" **JP McDonald, author of The Invisible Tether.**

VIROZONE

SARAH COLE

First published in Australia in 2021 by Little Steps Publishing

Printed in Australia

Cover and internal design by Shawline Publishing Group Pty Ltd

Second printing: March 2024

Shawline Publishing Group Pty Ltd

www.shawlinepublishing.com.au

Second edition ISBNs as follows:

Paperback - 978-1-9231-0165-4

ebook - 978-1-9231-0166-1

Hardback - 978-1-9231-0187-6

Distributed by Shawline Distribution and Lightning Source Global

A catalogue record for this work is available from the National Library of Australia

VIROZONE

SARAH COLE

For Chippa, Ros, Matt, Ethan, Alex,
Daniel, Nanny and Gran.
Thank you all, always.

CHAPTER 1

I PRESSED MY FACE up against the dome and peered outside. My eyes took a moment to adjust to the dim light as I tried to focus on what was happening, unsure and hesitant. My breath clouded the glass and my line of vision as I wiped a small space to see through again. What I saw wasn't new; unfortunately, it was very, very old. My mother, backpack on, breathing apparatus covering her once beautiful face, running between those who would rob her and those who would kill her.

I ran my fingers through my long brown hair in desperation, pulling it up into a high ponytail and hoped she would make it back inside AirZone alive. I hated myself for allowing her to run the line. Basically, whoever 'runs the line' is responsible for trading with the other zones to survive. We trade what we have plenty of, and for our zone it is air. The other three zones are divided into fire, water and soil. The essential elements for life are divided and cultivated within their own individual domes. We don't live well mind you, but we survive.

Then there is the fifth zone, *the Prestige Zone*. The Prestige or PreZone was just like it sounded: rich, better, perfect. Certainly, they were segregated in their own dome like our zones; Air, Fire,

Water and Soil, but PreZone had it all – all four elements and more. They had a limitless supply of anything and everything that we kill each other for and I hated them.

Everything was *new* in PreZone, unlike here, in AirZone, FireZone, WaterZone and SoilZone, each subdivisions of our world, *Virozone*. That's just how it was here, old and ugly and there was no escape.

In AirZone, between the hours of 6pm and 6am there is no sign of life in anything, trees, animals, definitely not people, not after AIRLOCK curfew, except the Captors. They still scare me and I hate seeing them, so I rarely look out my window during AIRLOCK. During AIRLOCK, the Captors infiltrate each of the zones and steal what they need to fuel PreZone. In AirZone, they capture our air, stealing it for the Prestige and greedily saving it for themselves. The Captors are in fact men, but to me they are not human. In intimidating masks, complete with octopus-like tubes and spidery wires, which twist around their backs and attach to huge air bottles, causing them to hunch over, they look demented and frightening. They lurk around our zone, sucking up our air, skulking around our houses. They used to give me nightmares. Sometimes they still do.

But all of this wasn't new to me; I'd grown up with it. We stay in our houses, shut all the windows, doors and shutters air-tight, and use the air we have accumulated through the day, as we cannot have anymore. One day we will run out, but the PreZone won't, that's their grand plan: to take all of our air and live forever. I seriously couldn't imagine my life without Mum and my best friend, Cobin.

I'm sure the world wasn't always like this. Apparently, once upon a time, the world was one. No domes, real life assortments of living animals. It's unimaginable. A world where people actually threw away rubbish. Crazy, who would throw away anything? Yet as the one world slowly died, full of pollution and overflowing with waste, it was decided that the four elements: air, fire, water and soil be divided up to ensure they could be sustained forever. In doing so, four leaders were chosen and they were each given the responsibility of their zone and to ensure it flourished. But even that didn't last long. There were those who wanted more, wanted to have more than others, and that was when the war to end all wars took place. The 'Enmity' lasted one year and three days. The outcome being four dead leaders and a brand new fifth zone: the 'Prestige Zone' or 'PreZone'. Virozone was no longer run by four independent zones, but by one, ruled by one leader, and his name was Sceptre.

My mother flashed her AirZone I.D. Brace against the security lock as she entered the AirZone. Each zone had their own individual I.D. Brace: AirZone was yellow, SoilZone: brown, WaterZone: blue, and FireZone: red. But the Prestige Zone I.D. Brace consisted of all four colours. The only difference between a male and female's is the shape of the individual buttons: male, square and female, diamond. All I.D. Braces have the same two buttons, one identity information and the second - evaporation. You could not enter a zone without the correct I.D. Brace, thus keeping us undesirables out of PreZone permanently.

Neither Mum nor I had ever experienced an evaporation – a simple press of the diamond button on your I.D. Brace causing you to black out temporarily. Certainly, I knew about the permanent evaporation, the removal of your I.D. Brace from your wrist by either yourself or another, causing you to evaporate, meaning you dissolve and disappear into nothing and are no longer there, here, anywhere. You are gone. But it isn't all bad, there is a chance that you can remove your I.D. Brace at any time and give it to another, hence sacrificing your life for theirs. But this was rare and I wasn't entirely sure that I could ever accept one, or give mine away, so I tried not to think about it.

Instead I watched my mum walk through the AirZone opening. I had stopped pretending that I wasn't waiting nervously for her a long time ago. Now I just hugged her even tighter as she released her mask and smiled at me.

'Waiting again, Lawlie? Couldn't you be doing something more important, like compressing air for my next run?' She squeezed me tighter and I knew she was secretly glad I missed her, after all, it was just us.

'I'm just waiting for news about the next Burning of the Light Ceremony. Sceptre is supposed to announce the sacrifice today.'

'You know I hate that stuff, Law. It's really disgusting that Sceptre feels he needs to sacrifice someone from each of the zones in order to keep his power alive.' Walking home I glanced over at AirZone's community Double U screen and watched images of PreZoners laughing and smiling as they enjoyed all the elements that we were not privilege to.

The ceremony dated back years and was a symbol of the Prestige's power and all that they stood for. They find someone poor, someone worthless, yet strong and determined. They need to be a leader, a voice, someone any zone would follow and love, someone who could destroy the PreZone if given the opportunity.

The Prestige wait until midnight, lay the sacrifice on the ancient altar and have them evaporated into nothing, as if they were nothing and could never be something. It's recorded live and streamed into all of the zones via Double U screen for all to watch as a warning that the Prestige, the PreZone is in control always.

Opening the front door to our house, I immediately sat down on our couch as Mum unloaded her backpack. 'What did you get this time?'

She placed three bottles of water on the table and a large bag of dirt. She looked sad as she opened the bag and sniffed it. 'Could only make the two zones; Soil and Water. Fire was just too busy. You know how it is coming into winter, they must do an amazing trade.' I took the bottles of water into the kitchen and put them into the fridge.

'Air is pretty important too, Mum, don't forget that.'

She forced a smile, 'I'm just so tired of living like this, Lawlie. The runs are getting more and more dangerous. I saw three people getting mugged today for their supplies and I didn't even think to try to help them.' Of course she couldn't save them, no one could or really, no one *would*.

I watched Mum closely as she scratched at her spiky brown hair, both of us not having showered for a couple of days. My hair felt greasy, pulled back into a rough ponytail, but we couldn't waste our water. We knew water was to be saved first and foremost for drinking. She placed the bag of soil on the floor next to a couple of new pots, perfect for growing our potatoes over the next couple of months. I continued to move the water around in the fridge, making room for the new bottles, when a familiar voice interrupted my sorting.

'Hey, Law. I saw your mum come in. Oh hey, Helen.' I poked my head out from the fridge; it was Cobin Tucker, my best friend.

5

I told him he was only my best friend because I had no others. But really it was because he could make me laugh even at the most awful times. With his floppy blonde fringe that mostly covered his large blue eyes, he was wearing his usual green hooded jacket and ripped grey jeans.

So, how do I begin to explain Cobin Tucker? I suppose I should start with when we met. I was five years old and he was five and two months, a fact that he never lets me forget. I'd had a fight with Mum and had decided to run away. I made it as far as Cobin's front yard, just as the AIRLOCK warning sirens began to sound.

Mum was beyond worried, racing around to the neighbourhood houses, screaming and howling my name. Everyone was already sealed in and she had no one to help her, except Cobin. He had seen the whole thing from his bedroom window, so, at just five years and two months, he unlocked his window frame, climbed out and started yelling, 'She's here, she's here hiding.' He was wildly pointing at me, hiding in his family's garden bed. I was all scrunched up and clutching my tiny backpack, hoping to not be seen. I looked up and saw him hanging out his window, just as Mum scooped me up into her arms and into his house with two minutes to spare. Mr Tucker, a huge man with a soft, round face and Cobin's cheeky smile, let us in and we stayed the night until the AIRLOCK had subsided. It was a big risk for the Tuckers to take, sharing their air with two more people when they might have only had enough air for themselves. According to Mum and Mr Tucker, Cobin and I stayed up most of the night talking, and it was then that he coined my nickname, 'Spare'. He reminds me to this day that he saved me, became my spare air, and that night we made a promise that we would always be there as each other's spare air. Thankfully, since then, we've never had to be.

I smiled at Cobin as I closed the fridge door, 'Hey Cobe I–'

SMASH!

We both jumped, scared, alert, shocked. Running to the window I looked out apprehensively. The sky was streaked red and black, which only meant one thing: AIRLOCK. Every so often AirZone was put into AIRLOCK without warning, PreZone randomly shut down our air and sent in the Captors. Most of the time a few of the unlucky AirZone residents would be trapped outside their house, unable to make it inside and would suffocate. It didn't bother the PreZoners if a few of us died, they'd be happy if all of us just vanished, and maybe that was their plan.

'Quick Cobe, shut the doors, lock them, check the windows. Where's Mum?' Mum had disappeared without me noticing. I shouted out, loud enough for her to hear, 'Mum AIRLOCK's on, come back!' Cobin and I frantically began running around the house, Cobin locking all the openings, while I searched for Mum.

She was missing.

My voice was getting more desperate as I shouted out for her in fear. I pulled back the curtains and searched outside through the lounge window. It was three minutes until lockdown. She was just inside, where could she have gone?

Two minutes until AIRLOCK.

'MUM!' I screamed as loud as I could, knowing it would never be loud enough. Cobin had locked all of the doors and windows and was staring at me, waiting for further orders.

'I don't know Cobin, I don't know what else to do!' I was yelling at Cobin, like a wild animal, howling for dear life.

One minute until AIRLOCK.

I didn't know where else to look or what to do. I cursed Sceptre for the AIRLOCKs.

Thirty seconds until AIRLOCK.

Cobin and I both jumped at the sound of loud banging at the door. 'What?' I turned to Cobin. He shrugged and we raced to the door. It was Mum. I unlocked the bolt on the door and swung it open, pulling her inside by her arms. Slamming the door behind her I locked the door and spun around.

AIRLOCK.

Outside it was jet black and still, no air, the AIRLOCK had begun, and who knew just how long it would continue. I closed the curtains, not wanting to see any Captors slinking around, taking the air I was breathing not ten minutes ago. Mum was staring at me with wide eyes as I yelled at her, 'What were you thinking? Why were you even outside? When did you leave? Don't you know you could have died?'

Mum looked slightly shaken and sat down on the couch. 'I didn't realise. I—I had no idea. I must have wandered off. I'm actually not feeling that well.' She was holding a half empty bottle of water as I stood over her with my hands on my hips. She didn't look how she normally would, she was vague, confused.

I softened a little and sat down beside her, 'Maybe the run was a bit much for you this time, Mum, maybe you need a rest.' She looked at me shaking, her eyes tired but she didn't respond.

Cobin came into the living room and sat down on her other side. He raised his eyebrows as if questioning me and I just shrugged. Eventually she looked up at Cobin and spoke, 'Hello Cobin, how is your father doing?' Cobin looked confused.

'What do you mean? Wasn't he supposed to be with you?'

My mother stopped still and bit her lip, her brown eyes widened in shock. 'No, I thought that was next week. We said next week not today. Unless I got it wrong?'

Cobin's eyes shot from Mum to me, 'He left to meet you ages ago and I haven't seen him since. He was going to your usual meeting spot. Unless—'

I grabbed Cobin's shoulder and pressed my hand over his mouth. 'Don't even say it. He'll be fine, he would have just realised Mum wasn't there and gone on the run himself. He's probably just running late. Mum said it was packed today, right?' I tried to sound convincing, but the tremor in my voice betrayed me.

Cobin backed away, mumbled something, took a deep breath and ran out the door. Mum and I stared at each other as she continued to chew on her bottom lip. She was the first to speak.

'I really thought we were supposed to meet next week. What if—' I shook my head slowly at her, trying to make her stop before she finished her sentence.

'No Mum, Mr Tucker will be fine. He's experienced and strong. If you can get through, he certainly can.'

Mum shook her head. 'Don't you see, Law? Because he can carry so much more than me, it makes him a bigger target. You should see some of the looks he gets from the Desperate out there. I just hope that if it comes to it he gives them what they want and comes home.'

I didn't really have anything to say that would fix the situation. We both knew the dangers of the run and also knew that we had no choice. The Desperate are those who had lost all hope in civilisation, who would hurt anyone for anything at any time. I just wished I was older so Mum would let me go instead of her, but she flat-out refused, even though I asked every single day.

'I think I'll go over to Cobin's and see if I can help, or at least calm him down.' Mum nodded, although she was clearly lost in her own thoughts, no doubt blaming herself for the entire miscommunication.

'Okay, just be back for dinner.' I squeezed her thin arm on the way out, took a deep breath, and opened our front door quietly. Cobin's house was directly across the road, so it didn't give me long to think about how I could help or what I would say.

His front door was closed but unlocked and Cobin was pacing around the kitchen. When he saw me he stopped and spoke, 'I wish Jewel was here. She'd know what to do.'

I shrugged, knowing that was impossible, 'I told you you'd need your big sister one day, Cobe, and that her moving to WaterZone and marrying Marcus was a big deal.'

Cobin's eyebrows frowned, 'Yeah, well I guess it made trade easier for us both, having the connections between the zones, but I need her now, and she's not here.'

'Well I am here, you've got me.' Cobin stopped pacing and shot me a somewhat thankful look, but I knew how he felt.

Other than Jewel, it was just Mr Tucker and Cobin. His mum died when Cobin was little from a mugging in the Void. They ripped her breathing apparatus straight from her face, stole her air canisters and left her to die. Cobin had never really got over it, although he was just three at the time. I know he still struggles with her loss.

I walked over to him. 'He'll be okay, Cobe. He's smart and brave. Really, he's the complete opposite of you.' I tried to make a joke, but he just smiled half-heartedly.

He stared at me and spoke fiercely, 'I'm giving him another hour and I'm going out there.'

I pushed him back roughly, 'No you're not, Cobin Tucker. You have never even been out of AirZone and your dad would never, ever want you to go after him, not ever.' He shrugged at me, clearly his mind was set.

'He'd go look for me, Law. He could be lying somewhere injured, mugged, beaten. He could be dying. They might have stolen more than his goods, they might have taken his breathing apparatus just like–' I shoved my hand over his mouth for the second time that day. I was actually getting quite good at cutting him off.

'No. Not like that. Never like that.'

Tears started to seep from his huge blue eyes as he sat down at the kitchen table. He put his head in his hands and asked, defeated, 'What else can I do? I can't just wait here forever. If it was you, Lawlie Pearce, you would go. You'd already be gone.'

I sat down next to him and put my arm around his skinny shoulders, 'This isn't about me Cobin. It's about you. Your dad would definitely not want you out there. It'll be dark out in the Void soon and you know it is so much worse at night. Just look out the dome if you don't believe me, it's terrifying.'

He knew I was right. He knew exactly how scary the Desperate could become out in the Void if they hadn't gotten anything running the line. The Desperate were more than just those living out in the Void, lurking amongst the nothing between the zones, they were killers. In the darkness they could kill and steal and return home as if it was nothing at all.

'I can't just wait here, Law. It's been too long. You know how long a run for Dad usually takes. He's been gone for ages and I'm worried. I can't just stay here waiting for him to return.' He stood up and grabbed his backpack from the floor and began loading it up with bottles of water. He filled his pockets with four packets of matches and finally looked down at me still sitting, frozen at the old table.

'I know what I'm doing, Law. I've seen Dad do it a million times; spoken to Jewel about it over a hundred. I'll just keep my head down and move quickly. There are only the four zones, three if you don't count ours.'

I stood up and glared at him with angry green eyes, 'I hate you, Cobin Tucker. I hate you.'

His face softened for the first time in hours as he tilted his head slightly to the side. 'Why, Law? Because I'm doing something I should have done hours ago?'

I stalked over to him and stood up on the balls of my feet, facing him eye to eye, 'No, Cobin, because I'm coming with you.'

CHAPTER 2

'HOW ARE WE GOING to do this, Cobin? I mean, we don't exactly know where to find your dad, and let's be honest here, we have never left AirZone.' I could tell Cobin didn't care, and if I was him I wouldn't either. But I'm not him, and I think stuff through, especially big stuff like this.

'It can't be that hard. I mean, we've looked out our dome before, we've seen the roads, the signs. People run the line every day and manage to survive. Some more than others, but still, I figure we just follow the signs.'

Once the AIRLOCK was over, Cobin walked me out his front door and to the letterbox, where we finalised our plan. I was to tell Mum that Cobin's dad had made it home safely and that I was spending the night at his house. This wasn't unusual for us, so Mum wouldn't question it too much. We often went several days in a row without seeing each other, even when she wasn't on a run. There was always work to be done and the more allies you had, the better off you were.

'Hopefully she won't want to see your dad and just lets me go. She's always pretty tired after doing a run and falls asleep early. Do you promise we'll be back soon?' Cobin shrugged and looked around sadly.

'You know I can't promise that, Law. But I can hope – we can hope that we'll be back soon. That's the best I can give you.' He was right. It was impossible to predict what was out there, who was out there. But I couldn't let him go on his own, not now, not ever.

I knew that if Mum found out what we had planned, she would lock me in the house until I was twenty. So it was far easier to lie and pretend Mr Tucker had arrived home safely, but the thought of it made my stomach churn. I never lied, especially not to Mum.

Walking back through my front door, I began to unload my lies as Mum sat counting some seeds she'd accumulated, 'Saw Mick, Mum, he's all good, just got lost a bit.'

'Oh, I'm so glad Mick made it home. Are you sure he doesn't need anything? Did he say how the run went? Maybe I should go over and see.' I stopped still with my backpack on, full to the top with my BA, two bottles of water and some fruit.

'He actually said he's really tired and just wants to rest. He said it'd be perfect if I stayed over and could help Cobin load some air canisters for later in the week.' Liar.

'Okay, well make sure you apologise for me for the mix-up and tell Mick that I'm still fine to go with him next week.' Mum began filling her new pots with her newly acquired soil and seeds and knew I was safe across the road. Although I was crushed inside for lying to her, I also knew I couldn't let Cobin go out into the Void alone. He was hopeless, and at least I could navigate.

'Mum? I'll see you soon, okay?' I tried to hide the trembling in my voice, I never cried and I wasn't about to start now.

She looked up from her spot on the couch. 'Love you, hun, see you soon.' I smiled, paused and gave her a hug. After all, I might not return, there was just so much that could go wrong.

But wasn't that just how my life was now? Not having ever known my dad I certainly didn't have a lot of family and friends. Unlike Cobin, who at least had his sister and hopefully still his dad. I often asked Mum about my dad, especially when I was younger and all she'd given me was a story about him moving to another zone. I pressed for details, for dates for times, for any information that could help me figure out why he would leave us, but my mum was stubborn and wasn't going to budge, ever.

Sometimes I pretended he was some great hero hiding out, waiting for just the right time to take down the zones and re-set the world. Maybe that's what he was doing? All I have to remember him by is a necklace he left on my bedside table when I was four, before he left twelve years ago. My necklace, a small silver circle encased with silver moulded feathers, had become a kind of talisman to me. I touched it lightly now, hoping that one day I'd figure out what happened to him, or that Mum would tell me, whatever came first.

Standing in the lounge room watching Mum, I wondered what life would be like without the zone divisions. Would it be possible for the five zones to combine and simply work and live together? Was there really a need for such violence and hatred just in order to live?

I wondered though, what would happen if one day it was decided that the zones were abolished? I asked Mum once and she cut me off before I could finish my sentence. She said that Sceptre sends spies to listen to citizens' conversations and evaporates anyone who questions his rule. I told Mum she was paranoid and that Sceptre obviously had better things to do with his time, like enjoying all the privileges of PreZone, than bother about my lame ideas for the future.

But to my surprise, her forehead furrowed and she spoke slowly and softly, saying that the 'lame' ideas of a sixteen-year-old girl was exactly what Sceptre was afraid of. I never spoke of it again. But that doesn't mean I don't think about it every day.

'Love you, Mum. See you soon.' I had to believe I would be back. That's how I function, either believe in the positive, the hopeful, the good, or nothing. I reminded myself of that as I walked out the front door. As I entered Cobin's house I noticed he was already packed with his BA on his back, testing it out. I pulled mine out of my overflowing bag and asked him to help me assemble it.

'I have never used one of these before, only ever seen Mum do it. How do you know what to do?' Cobin shrugged as he clipped the small machine to my back and threaded the hose to the mask resting on my forehead.

'I don't, but it can't be that hard, right?' I rolled my eyes, of course he had no clue, and here I was risking my existence, as pitiful as it was, to help him.

I breathed out and pushed the mask down over my face, and the breathing apparatus over my mouth. It wasn't that different, really, I could still see and talk and most importantly, I could still breathe.

Cobin copied me and pretty soon we were facing each other, standing in the doorway of his house hoping that we would succeed. Staring at each other, we both burst out laughing. Not that the situation was at all funny, but with the masks tight on our faces, we did look ridiculous.

'You know I look better than you, right?' I said, fiddling with the straps on my machine.

He grinned, 'Of course you would worry about how you look!'

I shoved his arm. I certainly never cared about my appearance. What was the point? There was nothing I could do to change it.

'You look like one of those funny animals that used to live in the ocean, the one with all the legs. What was it called?'

He smirked back at me and retaliated, 'You mean an octopus. And you look like an elephant. If you even know what one looks like! You never did pay attention to that sort of thing in school.' I'd never seen the point in learning the names of long-extinct animals. What good did it do? I laughed along with Cobin anyway and then paused as a type of sadness crept in. I didn't like to think of the world as it used to be. It made getting through the day that much harder. Cobin and I stared at each other in our suits as Cobin pushed a stray bit of my hair back behind my ear. I reached up and touched his hand, and I didn't want to ever let it go. He smiled as if he understood exactly what I was thinking, because he was thinking it too.

We took our BAs off and I took the lead through Cobin's front door, when he pulled me back softly by my arm. 'Thank you. I mean it, thank you so much for coming with me. I'm really freaking out inside and knowing you're here with me, well, it's okay.' He moved his arm down to my hand and held it tightly. I squeezed his warm hand back and nodded.

'We got this, Cobe. You and me, let's go.' And with that, I led him out of his house, his life that he had always known and down our street to the opening of AirZone – the only way in or out. Were we ready? No, but we were going anyway.

CHAPTER 3

I GLANCED BRIEFLY AT the large, bald security guards standing at the entry to AirZone. It wasn't unusual for kids to run the line, especially if they were the only ones left in their family. Ultimately the guards didn't care. Leaving is at our own risk. All they cared about were those trying to get into AirZone and making sure they had a pass.

Exiting the dome, BA in place, the first thing I noticed was how the air had changed. Well, not so much changed but disappeared entirely. I could no longer feel a breeze on my arms as I did inside AirZone. Instead everything was still – dead still. Except for those running the line. I should have expected the change as the only air available is in AirZone. Once you leave your dome, if something happens to your BA, you are dead.

There are no trees or plants or food growing outside the domes in the Void. There can't be, who would waste their supplies on providing for anyone else? And nothing can grow anyway.

Out in the Void, the roads go on forever, long and windy, some orange, some brown, but all dry and dead. No wonder everyone rushes to get back home. Living outside isn't like living at all. There are no lakes, no streams, no mountains, no animals, no nothing. If you were to ever describe the end of something, this would be it. End of the line. The Void.

Cobin took the lead. He thought that he knew the way to our parents' meeting place. But so do I, of course. They had described it to us enough times, and just as we thought, there were plenty of sign posts along the way. After all, if you were doing a run, you'd have to be quick and smart and the signs were designed to minimise lost time.

As I followed Cobin, I looked ahead at the crowd of people madly moving along the road. Some carrying baskets, others trolleys. One skinny man, older than Mr Tucker, was pushing a pram filled with his supply load under a pile of dirty blankets. I wondered what he had traded and what he had hidden in there. He was moving fast, refusing eye contact with anyone.

There was a couple yelling at each other through their masks, a short thin lady with matted blonde hair and a teenage boy with fire-red hair, cut short all over. The short lady held a large tub overflowing with water, gripping it tightly as the young boy swiped at it with his bottle, attempting to fill it up. She was screaming at him as he continued to steal from her.

Cobin grabbed my arm and pulled me to the side of the road. There we stuck together, walking quickly and inconspicuously. 'I feel like I know this road,' I said as we began our journey along the dusty orange rock road. The sign read 'FireZone: This Way.' I had watched the road obsessively from our dome, but I had never walked it.

I tried not to look directly at anyone, which wasn't hard, as they all looked exactly like us: faces covered and slightly bent over from the weight of their BAs. Everyone was walking in different directions and everyone looked like they knew exactly where they were going. Well, except us. I wondered if the short blonde lady had won her battle with the thirsty boy.

'I think if we keep heading down here, their meeting spot is about five minutes out of FireZone. I know Dad said there's a series of steps and he and your mum meet behind them.' Suddenly Cobin didn't sound as confident as he did back in the safety of the AirZone. I nodded, it was similar to what I'd heard and so far it appeared we were going the right way.

It became darker the longer we walked along the road, and the hordes of people we first passed were now thinning out. No one wanted to be running the line in the dark. We started to jog; we figured it might save us some time.

There were no clouds in the sky and we couldn't light a match to see, but the glow from FireZone produced enough light to see the path ahead of us.

'We must be close. Feel that heat from FireZone?' I could definitely feel the heat and see the faint sheen marking our way. This run wasn't so bad after all, I was unsure why Mum refused to let me run the line so many times. Then, I became sure.

'Stop right now, you two.' A tall, wrinkled woman stood in front of us, wearing an old BA and holding up both of her scarred hands. Cobin tried to walk around her, but she pulled out a large, long serrated knife.

'I said stop, you two little lovers.' I nearly choked on my mouthpiece. Who was this crazy old lady?

'We need to pass, get out of our way.' Cobin sounded surprisingly strong, and I certainly was not going to let this walking corpse stop us from finding his dad.

'Don't you realise I will die?' She was speaking in almost a whisper, like she was hiding from someone.

'We don't have time for this, old lady. I said move,' and Cobin pushed past her. As he did, she attempted to swipe at him with her knife. Dodging it quickly, he pulled me along after him and we ran, faster than we had ever moved before. We weren't scared, we were unsure, and that was worse.

Eventually we felt as if we had put enough distance between us and the old woman. We could make out the slight outline of a seat ahead and crouched down behind it. Only the light from FireZone illuminated our confused faces.

'What was that?' I asked, still trying to work out if the old woman wanted to kill us or help us.

'I think she was messed up. You know, one of the Desperate been out here too long. But that knife she has, where did she get that?'

I smiled and grabbed Cobin's hand. 'You mean the knife she *had*,' I said as I placed the knife in his hand, his eyes lit up.

'You stole it! Are you kidding? We've been out here for less than a day and you've robbed someone?' He was laughing through his mask.

'Hang on, she was trying to steal from us! Plus, we might need it. I'd rather have it than not have it.' Cobin nodded in response and handed back the knife. I tucked it away safely underneath my shirt, just in case.

Squatting down behind the seat, we looked around silently, trying to figure out just how far off we were from reaching our destination.

'I think we're pretty close, that heat is getting really strong and I remember Dad mentioning the steps. Is that them?' Cobin pointed to a large mound about half a kilometre up the road.

I shrugged. 'I dunno, but we should go anyway. Come on.' I pulled at his arm as we both walked towards what would hopefully be our final stop.

There was no sign of the crazed old woman and, apart from a couple of loose people lurking around, we felt fairly safe.

The mound was in fact a set of large concrete steps reaching about a storey high. They didn't lead anywhere, well not that I could see and there was no one sitting on them. I motioned for us to creep around the back of them and see if Mr Tucker was there. Hopefully only him.

Walking as quietly as we could we braced ourselves for what might be behind the steps. Brutally scarred deserters? Dead bodies, robbed and hidden? I tried really hard to not imagine any corpses, especially Mr Tucker's.

But as we searched around the back of the tall steps, we found nothing. I let out a deep breath, not realising I'd been holding it in anticipation for what may or may not have jumped out and killed me.

'There's no one here. Maybe we're at the wrong spot?' I asked Cobin, as he shrugged. I knew exactly what he was thinking without him uttering one word. Where was his dad?

But then, out of nowhere a familiar voice spoke softly to us, 'Cobin? Is that you, Cobin?' I spun around so fast I almost knocked Cobin right over.

'Mr Tucker?!' I spoke far too loudly and clapped my hand over my mouth. I didn't want to draw attention to us in the darkness.

'Dad!' Cobin ran over to him first and embraced him tightly. 'Dad, what happened? Are you okay? Why are you down here? Can you get up?' Cobin was hounding his father with so many questions that he clearly was in no position to answer. Instead, Mr Tucker just nodded slightly and slowly. At least he was still wearing his BA and he could breathe. He was alive. I walked over next to them to assess the situation.

Mr Tucker was half lying down against the back of the steps. Almost invisible in the darkness. His leg was stretched out and bent in a strange direction.

'Your leg, can you walk?'

He shook his head slightly and pointed at his leg, whispering, 'I was attacked. They bashed my leg with some wood. I think they were from FireZone. I dunno.' It didn't exactly matter who they were. We would never find them and we couldn't afford to waste any more time out here.

'We need to move, Cobin, before anyone comes back. Mr Tucker, you'll have to lean on us. It'll be slow, but we have no other options.' I was making all the decisions and I needed to be direct and I needed to get us moving. Cobin nodded in agreement and bent down to help his dad.

Mr Tucker groaned in pain. I could only imagine how sore his leg was, jutting out on an angle, and I was pretty sure in the moonlight I could see some bone.

I quickly propped him up on his other side and let his weight fall on me. He was a big man, but I was pretty strong and although it was awkward, it wasn't so bad. We started dragging him, limping along out from behind the steps.

'I'm so glad you're okay, Dad. Well, you know, mostly.' Mr Tucker smiled a crooked, wincing smile, but I could tell he was happy too.

'Thank you both. I didn't–' I cut him off, he didn't need to talk, and he certainly didn't need to waste his breath thanking us. We found him and we were on our way home and that was all that mattered right now.

We knew how long the road back from FireZone should take, but now that we were slowly carrying Mr Tucker it would easily take a lot longer.

Luckily, most of the Desperate left us alone, barely looking at us as we staggered past. We obviously looked as if we had nothing except the man we were hauling home, so really they just didn't bother. I'd like to think that I looked far too angry to mess with, but it was in all honesty that we looked far too pathetic.

'Cobe, can you lift Mick up a bit? He's getting a bit heavy on this side.'

Mick groaned, 'I'm sorry you both. I can't believe this has happened and after what happened with your mum.' I could feel Cobin tense up and look away as he supported more of Mick with his back and shoulder.

'It's fine Dad,' he muttered, refusing to make eye contact with either of us. I wondered if he was imagining the 'what ifs' of our situation and I needed to reassure him we would make it home alive. But as I looked around at the wasteland that was the Void, I wasn't so sure myself.

The Void, while being desolate and bare, still managed to expel a sense of life. A hungry, bustling, saddened life, but life nonetheless, and isn't that something hopeful? That maybe one day we can be rid of the divisions and the Void and just live like they used to?

'What are you smiling about?' Cobin interrupted my thoughts on the future of Virozone, almost annoyed that I wasn't fixated on the dire situation.

'Nothing really, nosey. Just that we manage to live, you know.

All of us in the zones. We haven't given up and we haven't wiped each other out. We are still here, and I guess that's worth smiling about.' Cobin jerked his shoulder abruptly to the left as Mick grimaced in pain.

'Or it could just be that I'm carrying most of the weight here and you're slacking off.' I came to an abrupt stop. He was not going to start accusing me of not lifting my weight.

'Excuse me, Cobin Tucker, just what is that supposed to mean?' Like usual whenever I exhibited any sort of anger towards him he usually backed down. I was sure it was that I reminded him of Jewel and many years of her bossing him around and calling the shots.

But before he could retaliate, a croaky, rough voice interrupted, 'What are you lot doing? Dragging a dead horse home?' I didn't want to get into any conversations with anyone, but this man stopped right in our path.

What now?

'Let us pass. We are almost home. There is nothing you want here.' The large man grinned, an evil toothless grin, as he pointed at Cobin's backpack. 'I'll take whatever you have in there and whatever you have, too,' this time he pointed at me and I curled my lip back at him like a wild dog.

'No. On your way. Now,' I spoke in a slow, steady tone. I wouldn't hesitate to end this man if it meant saving one of us. I felt the hilt of the knife still safely hidden under my shirt.

'Your backpacks now, little ones.' I rolled my eyes, this guy with his rotten teeth, bald head and flabby stomach was really starting to annoy me.

'Let's go, Cobin,' I said as I tried to lead both Cobin and Mr

Tucker to the left of the gross man. But as I moved, so did he, and he grabbed my arm, forcing me to drop Mr Tucker. He yelled with pain as he landed on his already twisted leg. Cobin leapt at the man grabbing hold of his elbow and yanked him to the ground as I jumped on his belly, hard. The man gasped in pain as my weight held him down. He tried to get up, but Cobin controlled his arms. I didn't really think about what I was doing but I pulled out my knife and held it up to his throat.

'I will kill you right here. I don't want to, but I will. We need to pass.' The man stared at me blankly, no longer smiling. He nodded quickly, showing that he understood.

'Now, we're getting up, we're taking our backpacks and we're leaving. Do not follow us; do not even look at us. I will give you one bottle of my water and that is all.' The man nodded again. We got off him slowly as I continued to hold the knife out in front of me for protection.

I reached into my backpack for a bottle of water and placed it on the ground. 'That is yours, now leave us.' The man scooped it up fast and ran, even faster than Cobin and I had run earlier.

'What did you do that for?' Cobin finally spoke.

I shrugged as we eased Mr Tucker back onto his good leg, 'Any of us could end up like that.' We walked on in silence until we saw our dome.

'Finally! Home,' Cobin whispered as we each showed our AirZone I.D. Brace to enter AirZone.

We pushed our way through security and were safely in AirZone. We could always tell when someone had suffered while out running the line, their shear relief once they returned home transformed their entire body, and today it was Cobin and my turn.

'Well, you lot look like you've had a rough time. Come on get over here, take a seat.' It was our AirZone Community Leader, Mr Squall, his grey hair fluffy at the ends, poking out at all angles. He was smiling with his three missing front teeth and wrinkled face as we shuffled our way over to him.

Mr Squall was sitting with another two old AirZoners, and they stood up as we carried Mick over and he took their seat.

'What on earth has happened here? Bet it was those bloody Desperates wasn't it?' the older man growled banging his hand onto his knee. I nodded, stretching my own back, relieving my shoulders from Mick's weight.

'How long is this kinda stuff going to go on for? It's getting worse out there. The other day I had to rescue old Mrs P, a couple of Desperates were trying to take her bags. Not that she has much anyway, just some air canisters that I gave her last year,' he continued, wrapped up in his conversation with us, but honestly, I'd heard it all before. I stood there looking over at Cobin, his face strained as he stared at his dad's twisted leg.

'Yes, I know what you're saying. There is no point in going out there alone – at least two, two AirZoners need to be together and they need to be tough. Us AirZoners need to stick together. Fair enough, we have our rotation roster pinned to the centre square in town, but we may need to get even smarter about our runs.' I wasn't sure who was more tired of the two, but they had both seen and done a lot for our community, and ensuring the safety of AirZoners like us, was their priority.

'If only that bloody Sceptre would allow us entry into PreZone, even for just a stop in to trade some of our goods–'

The younger one interrupted, 'But why would he? There's nothing we have that they need. They have everything, if only they could get rid of us, they'd be really happy.'

Maybe they were onto something. If the PreZone was to eradicate all the other zones, it would just be them living their happy lives. But I hoped that never happened.

'Come on you two, let's get me home and get someone to have a look at this.' Mick was trying to stand on his own as the oldies helped him again, Cobin and I sliding next to him underneath his shoulders.

'Oh my, what have we got here?' I recognised the voice without even looking behind me. Great, it was my mother.

'Hi Mum,' I mumbled as I continued to haul Mick along with Cobin's help.

'Hi, Mrs Pearce,' Cobin added somewhat sheepishly, knowing he was in just as much trouble for lying to my mum.

'Mick!' Mum gasped, almost pushing both of us off him and taking his weight herself, which she definitely could do.

'Woah, hold up Helen. I'm okay, they found me in time. I hate to think what—'

Mum bent down and investigated his leg, 'Yep looks broken to me, let's get you back to your place and we'll take a look at it.' Both Cobin and I glanced nervously at one another, hoping that maybe she would forget about our lies. There was no chance. Spinning around quickly she pointed her long finger at both of us, 'Now you two might want to explain exactly how you came to be outside AirZone and why I shouldn't ban you from each other for life, but I'll deal with that later.'

Of course, we had nothing to say in our defense, we had lied to Mum, and even though it was for a good reason, we both felt pretty bad about it. I breathed in and decided just to cop whatever punishment she gave us. I knew she would never separate Cobin and me no matter what.

Mum pushed us out of the way and supported Mick on the walk home.

She carried Mick into his house and laid him on the couch. 'Now don't you move. I'm heading back home to get a few supplies. I reckon I can fix that leg, well as best I can anyway.' I decided it would be best if I followed along behind and mentally prepared myself for the fight that was going to come.

But before I left, Mick grabbed my arm and whispered, slow and steady, 'Thank you. You and Cobin, thank you.' I squeezed his hand tightly and smiled.

'Just jump in when you hear Mum yelling at me from across the street, okay?'

Mr Tucker smiled, 'You got it.'

I told Cobin that I was going home to face Mum and try and take the blame for our lies, but we both knew he'd probably cop it too. She was returning to his house, after all. Cobin nodded and pulled me in close in a long warm embrace, 'Don't worry about your mum. We did it Law, we found my dad. Thanks to you.'

I shrugged, 'We did it together, you know. We make a good team.' He released me and I left out his old front door smiling to myself, and to anyone else who saw me.

CHAPTER 4

I OPENED THE DOOR, ready for another lecture from Mum and found her searching through her cupboard for medical supplies. A long bandage was crumpled up on the floor and I picked it up, folding it around in my hands.

'I guess I need to explain.' Mum didn't even look up, she continued to rummage through her stuff.

'I don't think you need to, Lawlie, it seemed pretty clear to me. You deliberately lied to me and left the AirZone, which I strictly forbade you to do, and ventured into the Void in search of Mick. Have I missed anything?' She threw two more long material pieces out into the pile.

'Yeah, but we had to.'

Now she turned around and with her classic mum face pointed at me said, '*You* should not have lied to me.' I should have guessed this is what she was most mad about, my lies.

'I know, but–' She continued to stare at me and I knew no excuses would be good enough.

'You could have died Lawlie, you both could have.' I looked down at the bandage in my hands. I had unconsciously twisted it into a tight knot.

'Well, we had no choice. You would have said no, you're always so cautious.'

'Oh really, and how am I supposed to be, Lawlie? You tell me. I'm stuck here in AirZone, fighting every day for water, fire and soil, trying to keep you alive. Meanwhile I'm trying to avoid random AIRLOCKs, Captors and the Desperate who try to attack us.' Mum's eyes were wide and her eyebrows frowned as she threw an empty air canister out of the cupboard and onto the floor.

'I'm sixteen, I can take care of myself. We found Mick and we brought him back to AirZone and survived, maybe you need to give me more credit for being able to take care of myself.'

She stopped what she was doing in the cupboard and stalked over to me with her hands on her hips.

'Okay then, you're so old and mature now. Tell me Lawlie, what will happen if you accidently get caught in a random AIRLOCK?' She was tapping her hip with her fingers.

'Well, I'd die.'

'Yep, and what if you get your BA stolen out in the Void? What will happen?'

'I will die.' Now I knew where she was going with this.

'Yep, and what if Sceptre finds you and decides you'd be perfect for the Burning of the Light Ceremony?'

'I will die. But—'

'Just stop Lawlie! Bottom line is you will die, and apart from me missing you greatly, I'll have no one to help me!' We stared at each other, our faces so close I could almost feel her breath and then we both burst out laughing.

'Great, Mum, so you don't want me to die because then you'll have no one to help you.'

Mum laughed again and pulled me in for a long hug. It seemed to always be like this. We'd both be angry at each other and somehow always turn it into laughter.

I spoke into her chest, still wrapped in her embrace, 'I'm sorry, we should have told you.'

'Yes, you should have,' she replied, kissing me on the head.

I pulled back a little and looked up at her, 'I won't lie to you again and I'll cop whatever you have planned for me.' Mum nodded.

'Well, you can start by folding all those bandages properly and then fill up some empty canisters, then start measuring how much water we have for the week. When I think of more jobs, that's what you'll be doing.'

I sighed and rolled my eyes, 'And don't bother rolling your eyes at me, you made your choices, now live with the consequences. Can you please grab one of the water bottles I brought in this morning? My throat is so dry from arguing with you!'

I smiled and hugged her again quickly before heading into the kitchen for her water. Reaching into the fridge I pulled out one of the newly acquired bottles and returned to Mum, fossicking through her cupboard again.

'Here you go,' I handed her the bottle and decided it was probably best if I just got started with my jobs.

'Well, I'll start checking our water supplies first, then get moving on the bandages.' Mum nodded, unscrewing the lid of the bottle.

'Okay hun, I'll be in here, still trying to figure out how I'm going to set Mick's leg. Oh and Law?'

I spun around, 'Yeah?'

'You did good finding Mick and bringing him home, really good. I hate to think what might have happened.'

I nodded, 'Thanks, Mum.' She smiled at me and returned to the cupboard as I walked to the back room and started counting our water supply.

* * *

I knew something was wrong as soon as I walked back into the kitchen. Mum was on the floor, on her back, grey liquid drizzling from her mouth. I ran to her, knocking over three pots and scattering dirt all over the floor.

'Muuumm! Can you hear me? MUM?' Her eyes were slightly open and she appeared to be looking past me rather than at me. I sat her up and more of the grey goo slithered from her mouth.

'Can you speak? Mum! What can I do?' She didn't say anything and coughed, splattering more fluid into the air and onto the floor. I looked around for something, anything to help her and I saw a half full bottle of water next to her. I picked it up and tried to pour some into her mouth. But she groaned, a loud animalistic noise, swiping the bottle onto the floor its contents leaking out.

'Noooo, it's bad, polluted. Don't drink.' I shook my head, unable to comprehend what was actually happening. She was dying, my mum was dying.

'MUM! Come on stay with me. I'll go get help, someone will know what to do.' I was shaking her, trying to keep her from blacking out. But she just shook her head slightly from side to side, as if knowing she was dying and there was nothing I could do.

'Listen, just listen,' she spluttered as she tried to get her last few words out. I put my head closer to her mouth, wiping the grey liquid away as it dripped on her chin.

'Your father, don't try to find him. He'll–'

'Just wait, wait here I'm going to get Cobin and Mick.' And I ran, flinging open the front door and sprinting across the road.

They were both sitting in their lounge room when I busted through their front door. Mick had his leg up on the arm of the couch and Cobin was sitting next to him.

'Help! It's Mum, she's dying, she needs help, quick!' Cobin was the first to jump up and lift Mick again, like before in the Void, and we both supported him on the shuffle back over to Mum.

It was Mick who got to her first, even with a broken leg and he started scooping big blobs of grey slime out of her mouth.

'Lawlie, get me something like a tube or hose, something I can use to syphon out this stuff. Hang in there Helen, stay with us.'

I ran over the cupboard, the same one Mum was going through before and looked around madly for something, anything that could be used as a hose. There was nothing.

'Quick, Cobin go to the bathroom, look in there, I'll go check.'

But Mick sat back slowly and shook his head, 'It's – guys, she's gone.'

Holding some random pieces from the cupboard I looked down at her, she had closed her eyes and the putrid liquid seeped further out of her mouth and onto the floor like a stream of silvery paste.

* * *

I sat holding Mum for what felt like forever. I couldn't move and didn't want to leave her, not again. Instead I just wiped her mouth and closed my eyes and cried. My tears fell over her face as I screamed and sobbed, I didn't even bother to wipe them away.

Eventually Cobin came in, I didn't even realise he and Mick had left. He crouched down and held me as I shook and howled like a wild animal.

Eventually I stopped and stared straight ahead. Cobin didn't say a word, he just waited for me silently, not letting me go and not moving an inch.

'She died Cobin. It must have been from the water bottle I gave her.' I looked up into his blue eyes and I knew exactly what he was thinking but he said it anyway.

'You couldn't have stopped it, Law. You didn't know, there was nothing you could have—' But I didn't let him finish, instead I jumped up, grabbed the half empty bottle of polluted water and smashed it against the wall.

'That Cobin, that is what killed her. Polluted water from WaterZone. Someone must have sold it to her and she died.' He grabbed my shaking hands and led me over to our couch.

'Okay, we know that can happen. These people they're desperate just like us and they can do awful things.' I stared at him straight in his face, he looked scared, worried about what I might do.

'Yeah, well this time, this awful thing, it happened to my mum and someone is responsible for that and I am going to find out who.' I stood up and started searching for my backpack and BA. Where had I put it?

But Cobin stood in my way, 'Not now, Law. Your mum, she's still on the floor. Come on, let me get some help and we'll bury her properly.' He was speaking slowly and reasonably, but I was not ready to be reasonable.

'Help? Help from who, Cobin? Your injured dad who can't even move? Or your sister who left you both and moved to WaterZone?

No wait, maybe we'll ask my dad. Oh no, he left too.' At the mention of my dad, I remembered Mum's last couple of words. What did she mean, don't try to find him? Why would she say that? Did she know where he was?

I wanted to unpack it further, but Cobin interrupted my thoughts. 'Alright, be angry, you have every right to be, but it still doesn't change the fact that we need to do something with your mum. She can't stay like this Law.' I tried not to look at her, I didn't want to see her again lying there covered in grey liquid. I just wanted to forget it. But as I turned my head and saw her face, I fell to the ground.

I couldn't move, actually couldn't get up. I just curled in a tiny ball and closed my eyes as hard as I could. I guess it was shock, I'm not sure. Cobin handled everything.

'She's in here, Mr Squall, in her kitchen.' I woke up to Cobin's voice speaking to our Community Leader.

'Oh no, not her mother.' Mr Squall spoke softly, almost to himself when he saw Mum for the first time. 'Okay, Cobin I'll need you to grab her legs, I'll get her arms, we'll take her to my place. I've done this before, too many times.' Cobin was nodding I think,

I didn't see, I just stayed in my safety position, my eyes jammed shut.

After a few moments they had left, and I squinted through one eye to make sure they were gone, my mother was gone.

I'm not sure what time Cobin returned, but he just laid down behind me on the floor and put his arm around me tight. He was warm and I could smell his sweat. I knew he'd help me and right now, tough girl or not, I needed help.

We stayed there until morning when light started to creep

through the kitchen window. I hadn't moved and Cobin hadn't let go, not once. Maybe he didn't sleep.

'Law, are you, I mean—'

I nodded and replied, 'Yeah, I'm okay. I'm not fully okay, but compared to last night I am alright.' I stretched and he moved with me as we both sat up and faced one another.

'Thank you, Cobin, for staying with me. Is Mum…?'

He nodded, 'Mr S has taken care of her, good care, Law, he buried her last night next to his wife in his backyard. He said we can visit, you know, finalise it.' I looked sadly around the lounge room.

'I don't want it finalised, Cobe, I want my mother back.' He rubbed my arms and smiled sadly.

'I know, but this is how it is here. You know that, we have nothing, then we have something and then nothing again. This is our lives.'

I was so sick of hearing how bad our lives were, how hard we have to work and how people we loved just die and we are just supposed to continue on.

I stood up, shaky at first, but quickly got my balance. I walked over to the fridge and found all of the new bottles from yesterday's run and began tipping them down the sink. Cobin simply watched from across the room.

'Well, guess I had better get to it huh? Start preparing for another run. I'll be running the line on my own now. Maybe I'll die, maybe I won't or maybe I'll be poisoned by some liar in another zone.' I was speaking far too fast and irrationally again, but Cobin just let me rant, he had seen all this before.

I picked up some old strawberries that were sitting on the bench. 'Oh look yum, strawberries, what a delicacy,' and with that I smashed them down into the bench with my fist. That was when Cobin intervened. He grabbed my hands and spun me around to face him.

'Killing strawberries is not the answer to your problems, Lawlie.' I managed a slight smile, he was right and strawberries really were a treat for us.

'What am I supposed to do now, Cobin?' I whispered, refusing to cry again.

'You can have Jewel's old space and we'll move your stuff in. You'll live with us.'

Looking around the kitchen, I didn't want to stay here any longer anyway. Every direction I looked, I imagined Mum and I couldn't face that every day.

'Okay.' Cobin's eyes widened. I didn't think he'd expected me to give in so quickly and was instead expecting a fight.

'Well, okay then, let's grab some of your stuff and you can move in right now.'

I found myself staring at the spot where I'd found Mum and without realising it, started speaking exactly what I was thinking, 'I'll move in with you Cobin, but it'll be after I do a few things.'

He frowned in confusion, 'After you do what things?'

I stared at him, directly in his big blue curious eyes and replied, 'After I go to WaterZone and kill whoever sold my mother that bottle of polluted water.'

CHAPTER 5

IT WAS MID-MORNING THE following day when I had almost finished packing my bag. I headed to Death Creek to release some of my anger and visit Mr Squall. The name Death Creek was apt, as there was no longer anything alive in or around it. It wasn't too far from my house and usually it would take a little over ten minutes to get there. Today it took me just five.

Death Creek wasn't as empty as it sounds though. Besides being home to our AirZone community leader, Gerald Squall, or Mr S, his five workers also lived there, each of them managing relations between us and the other zones. Here in Death Creek, the AirZone Community Leadership made all the major decisions for AirZone. I guess we are lucky, Gerald and his group always include us and keep us up to date in most issues regarding Virozone, they value our input and use it to negotiate supplies and trade and, of course, help in burying the dead. Today I needed to explain to him about Mum and state my intentions about uncovering the person or persons who poisoned her. I did want to seek his advice, although of course, I had already made up my mind.

I walked fast because I thought the faster I walked, the sooner all my anger would leave my body, but it didn't help. The creek had been water-free for as long as I could remember. I suppose at one time it was full, but I'm sure that was way before my time, and way before Mum's. There were random rocks, big and small scattered across the empty creek bed and I loved to shoot them with my slingshot.

Gerald's house was on the edge of the empty creek and his initials were carved into his door. As I knocked, I realised I should have probably brought Mick or Cobin along to support me.

'Enter,' Gerald's voice was as calm and clear as last night. I pushed the heavy door open and walked inside. I had been here before with Mum, and it looked exactly the same. Bare, with a long table, six chairs and a faded grey rug on the floor. Gerald looked up from his book and smiled.

'Good day, young Lawlie Pearce. How are you? Since last night, I mean?' His face was older than Mum's and wrinkled all over, but his smile made him appear younger and friendly. He was alone in his office, which wasn't that unusual, his workers would often be sent off to complete tasks, he was too old for all that now.

I took a seat across from him, 'You know my mum was killed last night. Thank you so much for your work with burying her. She drank some poisoned water from WaterZone. That's how she died.' I paused, and waited for Gerald to speak, but instead he looked out the window, as if checking no one was listening.

Then he whispered, 'Tell me exactly what happened. Don't leave anything out.'

I sat back in my chair and sighed, I started at the beginning from when we first realised Mick was missing, and ended it with him burying Mum.

When I was done, Gerald looked at me closely and closed his

eyes as if trying to remember something.

'Does anyone else know what happened to Helen?'

I shook my head, 'Only me, Mr Tucker, Cobin and you.'

He bit his dry old lip and breathed loudly through his nose, 'I am so sorry about Helen, she was truly a good person. But you know what this means, don't you Lawlie?'

'It means that WaterZone is deliberately trading contaminated water. But I don't understand why. Could they be trying to take over AirZone for themselves?'

Gerald nodded, 'Yes that's what I was thinking. You know this isn't the first time something like this has occurred. When we first split into zones there were several attempts to destroy each other; but that was before Sceptre, and I thought he had stopped all of that.'

'Or maybe it is Sceptre who is to blame.'

Gerald's eyes darted nervously from side to side, 'Shhhhhhh! You know you're not supposed to speak like that.' But he wrote something down quickly as he was speaking and motioned for me to look. I looked down, where he was pointing it read, clearly and simply.

I think you could be right.

After I had read his note, he screwed it up and ripped it into tiny little pieces.

'Well what now?' I asked, watching him put the tiny bits of paper into his drawer.

'Well, firstly we need to issue a warning to all AirZoners. No one is to drink any water from WaterZone without having boiled it first. Yes, this is a lengthy process, but considering what has happened, necessary.'

I nodded, following along with Mr S. I knew about the boiling process. It was long, but what choice did we have? The process involved all AirZoners boiling each and every last drop of their water prior to using it and especially before drinking it. It was really the only solution until we had the all clear that WaterZone, or Sceptre, was not messing with our water supply anymore.

'But what about me?' I asked and Mr S frowned.

'You'll need to boil yours just like everyone else, Lawlie.'

I shook my head, 'No, I mean, what do I do about WaterZone? I want to find out what's going on.' Gerald shook his head, almost too quickly.

'No, no, no, far too dangerous.' If there was one thing I really hated it was someone, especially someone as ancient as Mr S, telling me something was either too hard or too dangerous for me.

'No it's not. I can go to WaterZone with Cobin and say we're visiting his sister Jewel. While we're there we can break into the Waterboard and find out what's going on with our water.' My plan sounded pretty good to me, but I wondered if Gerald would allow me to go. Technically we needed a community leader's approval before any vigilante attacks.

Gerald's eyes faced upwards, as he began to weigh up the situation, eventually he responded.

'Okay. I will grant you permission to investigate – and only investigate – the goings-on at the Waterboard, and only because of what has happened to your mother. But I do not want you or Cobin Tucker employing any unauthorised attacks on WaterZone. Do you understand me Lawlie Pearce?'

I understood him perfectly, but that didn't mean I wouldn't do what I wanted anyway.

'Sure. I get it, no unauthorised attacks.' He continued to eye me for a full thirty seconds, as if he was trying to read my mind.

'Alright then. You go and get yourself and Cobin organised. My workers are out as we speak, rounding everyone up for an emergency community meeting. Everyone here needs to know the imminent threat they are under and the importance of boiling their water. I just hope I'm not too late.'

I stood up quickly, knocking my chair over. Picking it up I reached out and shook Mr S's hand, he smiled and nodded in recognition.

'I'll be back with the information soon. Trust me.'

His smile widened, 'Just come back and we'll all be happy.'

With that, I ran out the door to head home. But not before I did one final thing. I stood on the edge of Death Creek, it was dusty and brown, no trees or shrubs, as no one wanted to look after the area, so no one did. But I loved it here. Deserted and quiet, I could do whatever I wanted.

I pulled my worn slingshot out of my back pocket. I'd made it when I was ten and had been practicing with it ever since. I lined up some old pinecones. They were so old, the trees they'd once come from had disappeared long ago. I lined them up in a row on the edge of the creek and stepped far back.

I narrowed my eyes, took a deep breath in and fired a rock directly at the first cone.

BANG!

First cone down and out. I breathed again. BANG!

Second cone, disappeared. I grinned, knowing I had one left.

BANG!

Done and dusted! All three shot down in three shots. I smiled as I lined up some more pinecones for some more shots, never missing one. I wasn't really all that surprised. I'd been coming here for years, particularly when I was angry with Sceptre, which was a lot. But today I imagined it was Sceptre's head I was shooting at.

On my way home from Death Creek, I began to think about Cobin. He hadn't tried to talk me out of my plan. He knew better than that, and he would only be wasting his time. So instead he'd come with me to WaterZone. At least there we could stay with his sister. I was pretty sure he thought I'd get over my rage after a couple of days and once I realised how hard it would be to infiltrate a zone, but of course I knew me, and I never gave up.

'So, we'll tell my dad exactly what? That we're heading to WaterZone to visit Jewel and that we've been given the okay by Mr S to snoop around and see what we can find?' I shoved some old clothes into my backpack and I didn't care if Cobin was stopped by his dad, he couldn't control me – I no longer had anyone.

'Sure, whatever you think.' Cobin watched me closely. I knew he was worried about me, but I also knew what I was doing.

'Dad should be okay with Mr S checking in on him every day. He shouldn't need me for a couple of days.' Cobin sounded as if he was trying to convince himself, obviously feeling guilty about leaving his injured father. Mr Tucker was fine though, well, except for his messed-up leg. He was sad of course about what happened to Mum, and angry when we discussed the water, but then there was nothing he could do to change it – only I could do that. Anyway, we couldn't waste too much time crying and being sad here, there was just too much to be done.

Once I had my bag packed, I accompanied Cobin back over to his house. It wouldn't have bothered me if Mr Tucker had said no to Cobin leaving, I still would have gone, but he said it would be okay, and better than that, it would be good to visit Jewel and since he knew Mr S was behind us, he was supportive.

It didn't take Cobin long to get himself organised, some clothes packed, water, food, BA. We felt like we had been doing this forever, when we'd really only done it once before.

'I want to tell you both to be careful, but I already know you are. You're both smart and tough and I know you'll go straight to Jewel's place in WaterZone and be extra careful at the Waterboard.' He was right, I needed to go to Jewel's first. I needed to go there so I could gather as much information about the zone as I could if I was to find those responsible for killing my mum.

'Dad, you'll be okay, yeah? Mr S will check on you and you can kind of get around?' His dad laughed, looking at his leg propped up on the couch, now wrapped in a bandage. I couldn't see the bone anymore.

'I'll be fine and yes I can limp around. You go with Lawlie, but I want you back as soon as possible.' Cobin nodded and gave his dad a tight hug before he followed me out the front door. Cobin could certainly come home after a few days, but I would not be returning until I did what I had to do.

Cobin smiled at me nervously as we headed down his front lawn. Yes, it was all happening very fast, we only returned from running the line yesterday, Mum only died yesterday, and I had only just made the decision to seek my revenge.

I really didn't have anything to say to Cobin that he didn't already know, so I chose to walk in silence. He fidgeted with the zipper on his jacket and continued to glance at me every few minutes. I ignored his looks. On our way to the entry of AirZone, we could see the AirZone community gathering at Death Creek. I could vaguely see Gerald and his workers standing up the front, empty water bottles in their hands. I wondered if this would change the dynamic of AirZone, now that everyone was aware of the threat. Would community members turn on each other, stealing fresh water for themselves? I shook my head, rapidly trying to erase the image of AirZone turning into the Void.

Reaching the entrance to AirZone, there were different guards on patrol from yesterday. Today they were tall and skinny and again paid us no attention as we masked up our BAs and got ready to depart once again into the Void.

'How far to WaterZone?' I asked Cobin after we stepped back out onto the dusty road.

'About two days, I think. Further than FireZone, but I'm only going by what Dad has said, obviously I have never been there.' I didn't respond, I just looked straight ahead and began to walk, but Cobin grabbed my wrist. 'Are you sure you want to do this? Be sure, really sure.' I shook my wrist out of his grasp.

'I am,' I replied, and stormed off in front of him. Those running the line wore their usual expressionless faces as they attempted to sneak by unnoticed, but I noticed them. I noticed everything now.

The Void was busier than yesterday. It was morning after all, and not almost night. I led the way and Cobin followed close behind. We zig-zagged in and out of people as they pushed their wheelbarrows, dragged their trollies, and carried their baskets. Again I saw almost no children, though some were our age, I thought, but couldn't be sure.

It was hot today out in the Void. There was sun, of course, but the atmosphere was almost like steam, sticky and all consuming. I scratched my neck, not at anything, of course, there were no bugs, but I could feel my sweat dripping down my spine. We were only one hour into our journey and we had so much further to go.

'Do you want to stop soon for a break?' Cobin asked as he finally caught up next to me. I didn't answer him directly, I just shook my head and continued ahead. But he stood in front of me so I couldn't avoid him, 'Let me re-phrase that, Law. We need to stop. I feel like I could pass out. I need water.'

I screwed my face up at him and replied, 'Yeah, I bet Mum felt like she needed a drink of water too, Cobin, and look where she is.' He tilted his head to the side and I knew I had gone too far. 'Alright, let's find a spot over there.' I pointed to a barbed wire fence, half falling over on the side of the road. I was kind of relieved that we could stop for a moment, but only a moment.

I sat down on the rough dusty ground with Cobin beside me and watched everyone as they walked by. A few glanced at us, but mostly continued straight ahead. I breathed out long and hard and tried not to think about Mum, but every time I did, I just got mad all over again. But then something caught my eye. I looked over into the distance and saw maybe five people wrapped in a struggle. Arms, legs, feet and hands shot out randomly as they tried to punch and grab at each other. I could see a BA getting pulled off someone and a leg twisted in a strange direction.

'Cobe, can you see that?' He nodded as we both watched as they continued pushing, scratching, screaming and falling onto the ground. It was hard to determine from a distance if they were men or women, and what were they fighting over? Plenty of fights went down in the Void, but they were usually of the one-on-one kind – your commonplace muggings and arguments over supplies. Bigger brawls were almost unheard of.

'Do you think we should go help them?' I asked, half-heartedly.

'That guy they're thrashing won't last long. I can't tell, but I think he might be unconscious,' Cobin was already moving toward the fray and I sighed, following behind. I'd hoped Cobin would stay out of it, but no, of course not.

As we got closer, I could see that it was a boy on the ground. His eyes were closed and his BA was hanging partly out of his mouth. Upon seeing that, I rushed in, against all my better judgement, and stuck it firmly back in his mouth. Cobin grabbed his arms and I held his feet as we lifted him off the ground and pulled him to safety.

The fight continued, oblivious to us. The sound of bones breaking and flesh being ripped echoed in my mind as I tried to focus on the boy in front of me.

'Is he breathing?' I cried desperately at Cobin as he tried to find his pulse.

After a couple of seconds he nodded, 'Yeah he is, he's just passed out.'

Cobin emptied some of his water over the boy's face carefully. I moved myself in front of him to block the view from any passers-by who would gladly steal our water bottle.

The boy's eyes opened and he coughed loudly sitting up, wiping his eyes. 'Who are you?' he asked, as he looked from Cobin to me and from me to Cobin again.

'The ones who just pulled you out of that brawl over there,' I said as I motioned for him to look over to the fight that was still happening and growing in numbers. The boy brushed his curly brown hair from his eyes and looked directly at me.

'Thanks, I–I was just walking past and they trampled me, I

think.' I listened to him speak, but all the while knew he couldn't join us, we were in this alone.

'Do you think I could have a drink of some of that water you tipped on my face?' His light green eyes seemed sad and tired, and Cobin handed him a fresh bottle from his backpack.

'Thank you.' He lifted it to his lips and drank the entire bottle in one go. I had never seen anyone do that. Water was hard enough to come by, and you had to savour it.

'That's all you're getting, you know,' I said, trying to keep the shock out of my voice. 'Now that we're down half an hour and a bottle of water, we'll be getting on our way. Good luck.'

'Well, thank you very much,' the boy said, but there was something odd about the way he ended his sentence. Then in one swift movement, he jumped up, grabbed both our backpacks, left so stupidly sitting on the ground beside us, and ran. Fast.

I jumped up and started chasing him, but too late. Within seconds the boy had disappeared into the crowd, blended into the mass of BA-obscured faces.

I stopped still and breathed heavily, trying to calm myself to keep from wasting my air. Did he stage the whole thing? Is that what he does, fakes being injured to lure gullible runners? If so, it was a risky game. I couldn't believe I'd fallen for it.

I fell to the ground on my knees and put my head in my hands. It was over already, and we were barely into our – my – grand plan.

Cobin had caught up with me and was breathing heavily as he picked me up off the ground and hugged me tight. He didn't say a word, because let's face it, he didn't have to.

I allowed myself to be led out of the crowd and back to the barbed wire fence.

'I'm sorry, it was my fault,' I said as Cobin squeezed my hand tightly.

'Law, we both decided to help him against our better judgement. Let's just keep moving.'

I kicked the ground fiercely and orange dust flew into the air. 'How could we let this happen?!' It was already too late for us to return home – we had barely enough air to get us to WaterZone.

'It'll be okay,' said Cobin. 'We'll have to move quickly, but we've got enough air in our BAs to get to WaterZone tomorrow if we move now and possibly jog most of the way. Jewel will take care of us when we get there.'

I smiled at him and hugged him, 'Thank you. That is exactly what I hoped you would say.' He squeezed me back a little tighter than usual.

CHAPTER 6

AS NIGHT-TIME CREPT IN, it was difficult to tell if the air became colder or if the atmosphere of the Void was just becoming more chilling itself. I looked over to Cobin, 'It's time, we need to sleep at least for a couple of hours.' Cobin nodded and pointed towards a wooden hut, the sides were loosely nailed together and leaning off towards the left. There was no one in sight, so I shrugged and we crept slowly over.

I knocked on the door and, when there was no response, I edged it open slowly. Looking around inside, it was empty, a bit smelly but completely bare, no furniture, no blankets, but more importantly, no people. I sighed, relieved that there wasn't some crazy Desperate inside waiting to rob us or kill us, which would ultimately be much worse.

'What do you think this place is?' I asked once we were settled inside and sitting across from each other in semi-darkness.

'I dunno, I guess maybe a hide-out or something, a place to stay for a bit while moving through the Void? Kind of perfect for both of us.' Cobin smiled, but his eyes still looked around nervously.

'But what if someone comes back, Law? I mean it's empty now, but for how long?'

My eyes were starting to close and I knew I should try and stay awake, but I just couldn't.

'I'll do first watch then,' Cobin said, but I hardly heard anything as I was already snoring.

* * *

'Law, shhhh, wake up. Can you hear that?' My eyes flung open and I realised it was Cobin's face directly in front of mine. His eyes were wide as he motioned for me to stay still and quiet.

I could hear some noise outside the hut, low voices, maybe two or three – two men and a woman. Their voices were muffled and speaking quietly together. I looked around the empty room and realised there was nowhere to hide, nothing, we would be found.

I strained my ears to hear more.

A deeper voice spoke first, 'What you got? I got a couple of canisters, a few cups of dirt.'

Then the woman's voice, 'Yeah, I only managed to steal this from that hopeless old woman, and I don't reckon it would fetch much in a trade.'

I tried to picture what she was talking about, as well as following their conversation but it was hard.

The third voice interrupted, 'I reckon we need to hit something big, or maybe kidnap someone and try to sell them back to their family or to Sceptre for the Burning of the Light Ceremony.'

'Yes!' both voices said in unison and they laughed, cruelly. I bit my bottom lip hard and tasted some blood, we needed to leave, and fast.

I stared at Cobin wide-eyed and he made a sign with his

hands, the symbol to run. I clasped my own shaking hands over his and nodded. We had to run out, there was no choice and we had to do it now.

The door creaked open and we did not hesitate. Instead we bolted, together. I still had hold of his hand as we pushed past the three shocked strangers, caught off guard and confused.

'Hey!' I heard one of them yell, but I didn't stop and neither did Cobin, the blur that they became disappeared as we continued to run.

They didn't chase us, which was lucky, and they didn't try to grab us or steal our stuff. But it was at least twenty minutes down the road until we realised it was safe to stop.

My breath was coming fast, and I hoped I didn't use all the BA air before we got to WaterZone. Slowing my breath down, I looked around. We were still on the right track, I pointed to a sign: 'WaterZone: Five Hours', with an arrow.

'Who were they?' Cobin asked as we began our trek again.

'I dunno, but I'm glad we didn't stick around to find out. There were three of them and only two of us. It probably would have ended badly.'

Cobin shifted the BA on his face, looked at his air supply and nodded, 'Well, five hours to go, but we need to move. Come on.'

And with that we started jogging towards WaterZone, where we would be safe… we hoped.

* * *

Arriving at WaterZone, I was struck by how similar it was to AirZone. Both zones were located within huge domes with guards standing in the entrance, suspiciously checking anyone who wanted to enter.

'Pass,' demanded a tall skinny, mustachioed guard as we reached the front of the line. We showed our identification and they cross-checked our names on their list of approved visitors.

I was painfully aware that the air in our BAs was nearly gone as the guard slowly checked through his records. I knew that he would be unmoved if Cobin and I suddenly started suffocating in front of him. But finally he let us in, and nodded us towards a wide street called Waterfall Drive. Cobin pulled out the directions his father had given him and led the way.

I was too busy taking in the strange familiarity of my surroundings when I noticed Cobin taking off his BA, I leaped at him instinctively, 'What are you doing?! We aren't in AirZone, you'll die!' Cobin stared at me, surprised and I realised he was still breathing. I looked around, seeing the other people moving around me for the first time. None of them were wearing BAs.

'All of the domes are supplied with air from AirZone. I thought you knew,' said Cobin reassuringly. I could feel my cheeks growing warm. Of course I had known that, how could I forget?

'It's their tax,' continued Cobin. 'Every week each household must donate one canister to the dome and its distributed inside for everyone to breathe.'

I frowned as he spoke, 'But what if not every family can donate a canister? What happens to them?'

He looked away, 'You don't want to know. Let's just say everyone donates one canister a week. End of conversation.' We continued walking in silence.

Moving down Waterfall Drive, I looked around at all the houses.

It was exactly the same as AirZone. The same small houses and the same sad faces on those roaming around trying to organise their next source of food. Though one noticeable difference here was the use of garden hoses. Every house we passed had a hose and most people were using it either to fill up empty bottles or water their growing gardens. I thought about my mother and how precious small bottles of water had been to us.

'Down this street next,' Cobin led the way down Rainbow Avenue and we counted the house numbers along the way.

Cobin knocked on the door of number 32 and waited. All the houses on the street appeared quiet and empty. Eventually, a familiar voice spoke through the security door, 'Cobin, is that you?' Jewel swung open the door with a wide grin and embraced her brother.

'How are you, sis?' he managed to say through a mouthful of his sister's blonde curls.

'I'm fine, you know, same as usual, but you! What are you doing here? And Lawlie, you too? It has been so long, you're so grown-up!' She dragged us both by our arms into her tiny house.

'Tell me everything. How did you get here? How's Dad? Dad's okay, isn't he Cobin?' We sat down in the lounge room as Jewel interrogated us about her father and our journey.

Cobin took a deep breath. 'Dad is fine, but he's out of commission for a while. He was beaten pretty badly on a run.'

Jewel gasped, and I was quick to jump in, 'They broke one of his legs, but other than that, he's okay. Cobin and I found him and brought him back to the dome before he ran out of air.'

Jewel nodded, but still looked concerned.

She reached over the table and clasped Cobin's hand in her own and I smiled, it would have been nice to have an older brother or sister who cared for me, but now I had no one.

Cobin placed his other hand over Jewel's as if reassuring her, everything would be okay.

'Look Jewel, there's just so much to tell you. So much has changed since you left AirZone and now Dad's injured I think we need your help.'

Jewel stared at Cobin with her large eyes, not dissimilar to Cobin's. 'My help? How can I help, Cobe? Do you need me to come back to AirZone with you? I mean, what are you doing here if Dad is injured? Not that I'm not glad to see you, Cobe, but if Dad can't run the line...'

I knew what she was thinking. If Mr Tucker couldn't go out to trade for supplies, the responsibility fell to Cobin to take his place. How else could a family survive?

Cobin cleared his throat with a stony look. 'We didn't have much of a choice, Jewel. Someone has been tampering with the water that's being traded.'

'Are you serious? The Desperate will try anything. They do not care about others one bit, so selfish and, well, I'm just glad you both managed to get here.'

Cobin shifted nervously, 'No Jewel, I don't think it was the Desperate. The tainted water came from WaterZone. Someone here is trying to poison AirZoners.'

Jewel's eyes narrowed, trying to digest the information, 'You mean from the Waterboard? Someone from here is deliberately trying to kill off AirZoners, but why?'

Cobin looked at me and shrugged, motioning for my turn to jump in, and I did. 'I think they want to take out AirZone by poisoning us all and take the air for themselves, and they're doing this by killing us batch by batch from right here in WaterZone.'

I could sense Jewel becoming tense and defensive, she was a WaterZoner now and although she was an original AirZoner, her allegiance to WaterZone came first and foremost.

She removed her hand from Cobin's and crossed them over her chest. 'And what proof do you have, exactly?'

I crossed my own arms and leaned back in my chair. 'Well, they killed my mother for starters. What more proof do you want, Jewel?' I could see her face soften, she was tough, but I knew that she cared about me and Cobin.

Her tone of voice changed and she released her arms from her chest. 'I don't know what to say, Law. I mean, I've known Helen forever and that must have been horrible for you. What happened exactly?' Jewel wiped away a couple of tears, and she pulled me across the table into a hug as I filled her in on the details.

Once I had finished, she looked at both of us. 'So, what do you need from me exactly?'

Cobin shifted nervously in his seat. He loved his older sister, but she was not an AirZoner anymore, and that mattered. Would she turn against her own community to find the source of the poisoned water?

'We need you to get us into the Waterboard so we can have a look around. We think whoever is poisoning the AirZone water batches is using the board as their base.' Cobin froze after he spoke, waiting dramatically for Jewel's response.

'Well, Cobe, I'd like to help, but–' This is what I was dreading, Jewel refusing to help us and Cobin and I going into this alone.

'But what?' My arms were back, crossed against my chest. She looked at me and raised her eyebrows, unsure how to respond. 'Markus is one of the workers now, part of the leadership within the community. Imagine if I was caught with you both helping you spy on WaterZone.'

So that was her problem, Markus was somebody in a community of nobodies and she was scared. And I suppose she should be, Markus was her husband after all, and if she was caught and evaporated for plotting against WaterZone, he would be too.

She continued to explain, 'If we get caught we could be evaporated or worse, sacrificed, on live Double U screen in the Burning of the Light.'

I rolled my eyes, she was scared, but I wasn't, and I certainly couldn't allow her to be.

I grabbed her hand from across the table, like she had done to Cobin. 'We need you. There is no one else. Get us in there, whatever you need to do, do it and get us in there.'

My eyes locked on hers and I felt her warm hand twitch underneath mine as she looked from Cobin to me and back again.

'You know what the right thing to do is Jewel. You know.' Cobin's voice was clear and low, no more joking, no more light-hearted banter or loving words, he was dead serious, and so was I.

'I really would like to help, but, well—' I squeezed her hand and she snapped it back with a yelp.

'Lawlie, easy, you don't have to break my hand!' I continued to stare at her, but I didn't apologise. Where was the tough, fearless Jewel I used to know?

She breathed loudly in and out and finally spoke, 'Well, what do you need exactly and what evidence are you hoping to find? And exactly what do you plan on doing with this evidence?'

I felt Cobin's entire body relax a little, he knew his sister would come around eventually.

'We need to get in and get out with proof, find out who is poisoning the water meant for AirZone and we need to do it now.'

I smiled over at Jewel. 'So that's all, nothing really.' She nodded slowly, ignoring my sarcasm.

'If that's the best you two have come up with, thank goodness you came to me first. Here's what we need to do.'

* * *

'You need to get into the Waterboard, and to do so you need a distraction.' Jewel's eyes lit up as she formulated a plan inside her mind. Cobin and I listened, after all, she knew this zone, we didn't.

'I think I could help with the distraction. Give me some time to figure out just how I will cause it, but having everyone from inside the board leave, will only help in making sure no one – and I mean no one – sees anything.'

Cobin nodded at me and I smiled, this was turning out to be something alright. But I was worried for Jewel. After all, if she was caught, she'd be evaporated. If we were, we'd be sent back to AirZone and refused WaterZone entry permanently. But in the end, she had decided to help us, maybe she secretly had her own reasons. Maybe she would always be an AirZoner.

We didn't have anything to unpack since we had been robbed, so we asked Jewel how we could help out for the next couple of days. We knew that everyone always needed a hand and if we were staying there we needed to do our fair share.

'It'd really help if you both could head down the street and stop by the well, it's in the middle of our zone and basically where the Waterboard source their water to trade to the other zones. It's free for us of course, but I'll give you both one of my visitor passes so you can collect some for me.'

I felt a nervous thrill to be exploring WaterZone. It wasn't dissimilar to AirZone, but the noticeable focus on water was overwhelming. Cobin and I walked along the road and eyed all of the houses and streets in WaterZone.

'Do you think this is how AirZone seems to outsiders Cobin?'

Cobin shrugged and looked around. 'I guess, I mean this is their whole life, like air is for us. Wow, is that the well?' We stopped and stared at the huge stone circled wall that sat above the ground before us. There was a large, sturdy transparent fence built around it with notices that cautioned trespassers with an electric shock.

'I guess we get in over there?' I pointed to a large opening in the fence where a short, overweight man sat behind a counter. Walking over, I could already tell he wasn't impressed to see visitors.

'What do you intruder kids want, hanging around here?'

Although he was shorter than me, his aggressive tone, accompanied with bushy frowned eyebrows made me stand a little taller, hands on hips and about to retaliate, when Cobin jumped in, 'We're here to fill some canisters for my sister. Here's our pass and the paperwork you need.'

The ugly little man snorted as he looked over the paperwork. 'Right, go over there and line up like the rest of them, get what you need and leave.' I opened my mouth but Cobin shook his head and pushed me though the gate. Probably for the best. We didn't need to be kicked out of WaterZone on our first day, before I even had a chance to investigate the water situation.

'Just keep walking, Law. I know what you're thinking and don't bother. We have more important stuff to do.' I looked around at the people standing by the well waiting to fill up their own bottles and wondered if they'd all be as rude as the man on the gate.

'Hey, not stealing all our water, are you?' I heard a sarcastic voice from behind me, and I spun around, ready for a fight.

'If you have something to say, try saying it straight to my face. Oh–' I stopped mid-sentence as I came face to face with the same light green eyes and short curly brown hair from the Void. Yes, those same green eyes that had robbed us of our backpacks.

'You!' I grabbed him around the collar of his shirt and he smiled back at me, amused but unconcerned.

'Woooo, hang on a minute here, ease up! I still have your stuff. Yours and your boyfriend's?' He glanced towards Cobin, who pushed his chest out slightly, about to join in. I pushed the thief hard in his chest and he fell backwards.

I rolled my eyes. 'He's not my boyfriend. Where is our stuff?' The boy continued to laugh although he was on the ground.

'Wooo, easy, Law,' Cobin said, pushing his way in front of me, as the boy scrambled to his feet. Cobin began, 'Now, listen here, mate, we saved your life out there and you repaid us by stealing our stuff. Not cool at all.'

I elbowed Cobin out of the way. 'You better take us to get our stuff now. That's the least you can do. Without us you'd be lying dead without a BA, squashed somewhere out in the Void. Now where's our stuff?'

The boy sighed and reached out and touched my arm, 'Okay,

okay calm down. I didn't realise you guys were heading here. I didn't know you had relatives here.' He motioned towards our visitor passes as I shrugged off his hand.

I screwed up my face at him, 'Where are our backpacks?'

The boy brushed some dirt off his already dirty jeans. 'They're at my place. And don't worry, it's all still there. Do you want to come get them?' I could have seriously pushed him over again.

'Of course we do. Let's go.'

By this time Cobin had realised he should probably have said something and interjected, 'Well, why did you take it from us only to give it back?' It was a good question and who knew what was going through this guy's mind.

The boy shrugged, 'I didn't exactly expect to see you again. But here you are!' We walked out of the enclosure and down another street, forgetting about filling up Jewel's canisters. For now, getting our packs back was far more important. Looking around, all the houses looked the same – neat, tidy, empty and silent.

'Oh so you felt bad, did you, once you saw we were friends with someone from WaterZone.' I was stomping along, still angry and even madder because he was taking up some of the valuable time I needed here in WaterZone.

'Well, don't take it personally. I would have stolen from whoever pulled me out from that fight, it just so happens it was you and the chump over here.' The boy pointed at Cobin again.

'Look, come get your backpacks and have some food, then you can fill me in about what exactly you both *are* doing here.' We had stopped at the top of his street, Rain Boulevard. How did he know we were here for more than a visit? Were we that obvious?

'Well, we'll see. What makes you think we can trust you anyway?'

The boy smiled directly at me which showed his perfectly straight, white teeth as his green eyes widened, sidling up next to me he draped his arm casually around my shoulder. 'Because I think I might just be in love with you, gorgeous!'

CHAPTER 7

THE BOY'S LEG WAS grazed as he tried to stand up for the second time. 'You didn't have to attack me,' he cried as I continued to walk in front of him, next to Cobin, secretly pleased with my self-defense manoeuvre.

The boy began running after us. 'Aw, I was only joking! Can you stop attacking me every time I make a joke, please?' He was half laughing, half rubbing his shin where I had kicked him, and pretty hard, mind you, in my steel-capped boots.

It wasn't all that far to his house, which looked like every other house in the WaterZone community. He left us at the front door and, winking at me, he ran inside.

I could hear voices, I assumed he was talking to his mum.

Cobin motioned towards the house, 'What do you think about this guy?' I glanced at the door. He still wasn't back yet.

'I don't think anything about this guy, Cobin. I think we get our backpacks and we go about our business.' Cobin's eyebrows raised, but he chose not to comment.

The boy came back out carrying our two backpacks. 'Here you go, as promised.' I snatched mine out of his hand, shooting him another angry look.

'Thanks,' Cobin said. I wasn't exactly sure what Cobin was thanking him for, he did steal it from us.

The boy leaned against his front door with his arms crossed. 'So I reckon you guys need to fill me in. What are you two doing here in WaterZone?' I looked up from checking my backpack, everything was still in there.

'Visiting Cobin's sister. And now that we have our stolen bags, we will be leaving. Come on Cobin.' I grabbed Cobin by his arm and pulled him along with my backpack in the other.

The boy continued to stand at his old front door and I didn't care enough to check if he was watching us walk away.

Once we were out of sight, Cobin pulled his arm out of my grasp and skidded to a halt. 'Law, can you slow down for a moment? I need a drink and a rest. We haven't stopped since we left AirZone.'

I flung around to stare at him, my eyes flashing. 'Cobin, I'm just as tired as you, but we have no time and you know that.' I looked into Cobin's eyes, the same friendly face I had known almost my entire life and felt myself backtracking a little.

'Alright, alright, let's go over there. But ten minutes, that's all, and then we have to get back to the well, get Jewel's water and figure out the next part of our plan.' Cobin smiled and we headed over to an empty park.

The grass was green and thick, unlike ours in AirZone, I guess here they didn't have to conserve water. We took a seat next to some large bushes, it was nice to smell the fresh leaves and grass. I had almost forgotten what that smelt like.

Cobin pulled out a fresh bottle of water from his backpack that we had boiled before we left, and began to take a sip. 'Law, I dunno how we're going to do this you know. I mean, break into the Waterboard. If we get caught–'

I rolled my eyes, 'What do you mean get caught? I don't plan on getting busted and I certainly am not about to let whoever is poisoning our water get away with it.'

Cobin shifted nervously on the ground. 'I just think maybe it is too risky for us and for Jewel. I don't want anyone to be evaporated, Law, or taken for the Burning of the Light.'

I took the bottle from his hands and had a drink. When finished, I shoved it back at him. 'I guess it's easy for you to say, it wasn't your mum who was killed by drinking poisoned water.'

His head tilted on the side. 'Not fair, Law, you know I loved your mum too, but I also love you. You know, as a friend and, well, if something was to happen to us, to you–'

I pushed myself up from the ground but tripped on my backpack and fell backwards into the spiky bush.

'Hey, easy there!' A male voice came out of the bush along with two hands pushing me out. I screamed and clambered out, searching frantically for a weapon as the owner of the voice stepped out from the green leaves and I knew immediately who it was.

'You!'

'Well I could say the same thing, it's YOU and him again,' the boy said, pointing towards Cobin.

It was the backpack thief. I pointed my finger in his face. 'Are you following us?' My other hand was firmly plastered on my hip.

The boy brushed off some excess leaves from his jeans and smiled smugly. 'Well, not so much followed, but it just so happened to be that I was also coming here.' I rolled my eyes and put my other hand also on my hip.

'What did you overhear?' I knew he had probably heard everything, I just needed to know if he was going to dob us in.

At first he didn't answer and instead looked down at his shoe as he spoke in a lower voice, 'Look, I heard it all and I'm sorry about your mum.'

I relaxed my stance a little, he appeared to be slightly awkward. Was he embarrassed that he had found out something so personal about me?

Cobin interjected, 'What's your problem anyway? You go around listening to people's private conversations and stealing. You're bad news and we've had enough of you. Leave us alone.' I stood up a little straighter next to Cobin. He was right, we had been through enough.

'Yeah, just get away and annoy someone else. We don't need you.' I pushed him in the chest, hoping he would get the idea and leave but he just stood there.

'But what if you did need me?' His voice had changed. It was no longer the cocky talking thief from before, he was calmer and serious.

I replied, 'Well, I am completely sure that there is nothing you can give us that we need.' Cobin nodded in agreement.

But the boy just stared at us both, locking eyes and said, 'What if I can get you into the Waterboard.'

* * *

'Come back to my place and I'll explain everything. Trust me, would I lie to you?' He was grinning and deliberately teasing me. But shrugging at Cobin we decided to follow him anyway, apparently what he was going to say could not be overheard. I walked close to Cobin the entire way, fists clenched and ready to defend myself if this guy tried anything. Occasionally the boy would turn around and smile, but I continued to ignore him and it didn't take long for us to arrive back at his front door.

'Well, are you going to let us in or what?' I demanded as he smirked.

'Sure, come on. Oh and my name's Ryn, just in case you were wondering.'

I rolled my eyes. 'Don't worry, I wasn't.' Ryn laughed as we followed him into his house.

His mother had short brown hair and a slightly wrinkled face, and was dressed in black pants and matching top. She looked up from the kitchen table as we arrived, 'Ah so this is who you've been secretly talking to.'

I smiled a short, nervous smile, 'Hi, I'm Lawlie and this is Cobin–'

Ryn quickly interrupted, 'These are my new friends, Mum.'

She eyed him suspiciously. 'Ryn, are these the two owners of the new backpacks you acquired?'

Ryn looked at us, embarrassed and almost a little shy. 'They've got them back, Mum, now if you don't mind, we've got some planning to do.'

She stared at him and laughed. 'No trouble, Ryn, I mean it.' But she continued to laugh as she went back to her work on the kitchen table.

We followed Ryn to his room, which looked pretty much the same as Cobin's. Clothes on the floor, a few empty bottles on the table, a boy smell that seemed to never leave.

He closed his bedroom door behind us and motioned for us to

sit down on his messy bed as he sat on a swinging chair.

'So what can you do for us?' I asked, crossing my arms and looking over at Cobin, who just shrugged as if he didn't know what to say.

Ryn again motioned for me to sit down. 'Okay, well for starters, I can get you into the Waterboard to have a look around. A friend of mine, Sammy, she lives round the corner, and yes, don't look at me like that, I do have a friend.' I smiled. He had read my mind.

'She works for the Waterboard, you know, up near the well. Basically, they filter the water, check it and trade it. But last week she overheard some of the senior workers talking about some orders that had come from above, like Sceptre above. She thinks they were told to pollute a batch set for AirZone.'

I stared directly at him. So it was on purpose. My mother died from a poisoned batch of water. But why? Cobin interrupted, 'But why would they do that? What would be the point? To randomly kill some people from AirZone? I mean, why would their deaths be important to anyone but their families?'

Ryn bit his bottom lip as if thinking about possible reasons for the sabotage. 'Well, unless the polluted bottles were going out to all of the zones, not just AirZone. Then you would have poisoned people from each zone. Like you were–'

I interrupted, 'Like if you were planning a full-scale attack to take them out?' Ryn nodded in silence. So that was it? Someone, most likely Sceptre, had initiated an attack on each zone, to hurt them, kill them, wipe them out completely or turn them against each other?

'We don't know for sure. I mean, we're going to have to investigate this, right?' Cobin was asking both Ryn and I, but I'm sure he already knew the answer.

'Yeah, we're going to figure this out,' Ryn looked at me sympathetically. 'Before anyone else gets hurt.'

'So, now what?' I asked. 'There's three of us.'

Ryn, held up his hand. 'Four. We need to get Sammy. We need her, she's our way in and plus she's really smart.'

I looked at him. 'She can't be too smart if she's friends with you.'

Cobin held up his hands. 'Okay, okay, enough, you two. I can't be the third wheel in this never-ending feud. Can we just move on from the fact that Ryn robbed us and work on stopping any more polluted batches from getting out?'

I crossed my arms again and gave Ryn my most scathing look. Cobin may have forgiven him, but I wasn't so easily fooled. 'Let's just go see your friend.'

Ryn stood up and put his own backpack on. 'Right, let's go.'

I imagined that Ryn and Sammy were the WaterZone version of Cobin and me. As we arrived, there was a girl my age sitting on a seat on her front verandah.

'So who have you conned this time, Ryn?' The girl's voice was confident and clear as she threw some of her long straight black hair behind her shoulder.

'Sammy, you know me too well.' They laughed and she stood up and walked towards us. She was beautiful. Tall, slim, with her shiny black hair, and up close, tiny brown freckles scattered across her nose.

Her blue eyes seemed to laugh as she talked and she smiled immediately at Cobin. 'Hi there, and you are?'

I wondered if Cobin could respond. He looked like he might just fall over and die from even seeing such a gorgeous girl. So I interrupted, 'My name's Lawlie, and this is Cobin. Your friend

70

here did rob us, but has since rectified the situation. He said you can help us.'

She broke her gaze free from Cobin and looked me up and down, no doubt I looked the polar opposite to her.

'Well, nice to meet you both. I suppose if Ryn says I can help, I can certainly try. Let's get out of here though, I don't trust my little sister not to snoop and tell Mum and Dad. I reckon we head down to the Natury. It's this kind of nature spot made by the Waterboard. There are a few trees and a ditch, some soil, though obviously it doesn't last that long, as people steal from it a lot.' I wondered why the board would continue to re-fill the Natury if stuff keeps getting stolen. Maybe they want to live the illusion of how a normal, real life place used to be?

On the way over, Sammy tried to speak with Cobin. 'So, how long are you staying? You must have a relative here, right? Anyone I know?'

Cobin coughed and cleared his throat. 'Yeah, my sister, Jewel. We'll be staying there for a bit.'

Sammy smiled. 'Oh, Jewel! I know her. She always buys my mother's strawberries. I see her about once a week. I should have known you were related to her, she's lovely.'

Was this girl for real? Was she actually flirting with Cobin? I wasn't the only one thinking it, as Ryn decided to jump in too, 'Yeah, well let's get to the main info here. Sammy, Lawlie's mum was killed from a batch of our polluted water and she needs to find out who's responsible.'

Sammy held her hand to her heart and gasped. 'Oh no, so they did go ahead with it. You poor thing. Your mum, are you okay?' She sounded genuinely saddened by my loss. Maybe she was alright. Maybe.

'No, I'm not. But I will be when I figure out who is responsible and why.' Sammy nodded as we walked into the Natury. It was such a nice place. There were plants, huge trees, and bright green grass. We spotted a table and chairs located under a small tree and all four of us sat down. Ryn acted as the meeting chair.

'Okay, so now we've all met, we all know why we're here. Ideas?' I looked at Cobin, who was not so secretly looking at Sammy.

'Well, Sammy why don't you tell us what you already know about the Waterboard. Who did you hear and when?'

Sammy took a deep breath and began, 'Well I was working out the back of the factory, as Ryn told you, and I heard Skull giving some orders to one of the older workers to mix some liquid into the batches. That must have been how they did it.' We all sat there immersed in what Sammy had to say. I could picture the whole conversation and desperately wanted to hunt down this Skull person and kill him too.

'Who's Skull?' Cobin and I asked in unison.

'He works for Sceptre, he's gross. His face is tattooed to look like a skull and he rides this huge motorbike. He's scary, really scary.'

I held Skull in my mind's eye, all the horrible details Sammy had described in vivid colour. But instead of fear, I only felt rage.

'Well, new ideas, a plan, what do we do now?' It was Ryn again. We all looked at each other in silence and then I spoke clearly and slowly.

'We need to find Skull. We need to find out what he did and why, then, and only then, I need to kill him.'

CHAPTER 8

No one said anything for some time.

'Can't we just see how we go?' Cobin was always more cautious than me, but I wasn't about to let him just brush this off.

'Do I need to remind you that Skull poisoned the water that killed my mother?' Cobin looked away.

'Okay, Law, but let's just find him first. We don't know anything about him, or what he's really capable of. You can't do anything if you get killed too.'

I turned to Sammy. 'Could you talk to some of the Waterboard workers and see if Skull will be coming back?'

Sammy didn't look too convinced. 'I'm not sure. For starters, he lives in PreZone and hardly ever comes here. I can ask around though.'

'Can you really get us into the Waterboard?' I didn't care if she said no, I was determined to find my way in.

'Yes, I could possibly sneak you in.' Sammy sounded unsure, but committed at least.

The more I thought about it, the better the plan sounded. But it was Ryn who disagreed.

'Now, hang on. I just met you, Lawlie, and I don't know if you realise this or not, but you're not exactly a stable person from what I can tell. How do I know you won't do something crazy in there and put all of our lives at risk?'

I glared at him from across the table. 'Thank you again, Ryn, for such a compliment. But you don't know me at all, and frankly you were the one so interested in joining our mission. If you don't like it, you can leave.'

Ryn interjected, 'And how exactly are you going to get into the Waterboard without me and Sammy?'

Cobin and Sammy both stood up at the same time and Sammy stepped forward. 'Woooo, you two knock it off! All you have to do is get in and get out, all we care about is finding out what happened to your mum. Now, I'm working tomorrow and I'll let you in.'

We all sat down again in silence until Ryn spoke up again, 'Okay, so we just need to figure out a few details in case anyone quizzes us on why we're there.'

'Right, so let's get started,' I replied, staring him down, just letting everyone know that I could be civil when I needed to be.

Cobin looked over at Sammy, who was already smiling at him with her perfect smile. 'Me and Sammy don't need to be here for this right? I mean you two can just work it out and we'll just–'

Sammy interrupted, grabbing hold of one of the children's swings, empty and rusty, 'Take a seat here, one for you one for me.' Cobin smiled as he stood up and left us, quicker than I'd ever seen Cobin move before, as they sat on the swing set, swinging back and forth like they'd been doing it for years.

Ryn looked at me scratching at his brown curls. 'So, where do we start? What's our reason for visiting the Waterboard?'

'I think we should stick as close to the truth as possible. Someone robbed us, took our water supply and we need more.'

Ryn smiled and clapped his hands together. 'Perfect! That's actually perfect!'

I snorted out my nose. 'I've been known to have a good idea on occasion.'

He became somewhat serious, 'Seriously, Lawlie, I know you don't like me, and I don't particularly like you either, but here we are and now we're in this together.' I knew he was right but it didn't change the fact that I couldn't stand to be around him.

'Yeah sure, whatever, now I'm hungry. You want some lunch?' I unzipped my backpack and looked inside.

He looked up at me, surprised. 'Why what have you got?'

I pulled out a sandwich and a bright red apple and quickly zipped my bag shut. 'Nothing for you!'

I replied smartly, trying really hard not to hear Cobin and Sammy's conversation going on next to us.

* * *

'So how long have you known Lawlie for?' Was it my imagination, or was Sammy swinging extra close to Cobin as she asked him about our relationship?

Cobin laughed and replied, 'Is too long an acceptable answer?' Sammy laughed too, while I just sat there chewing on my apple. I couldn't believe how easily they were getting along, considering they had only just met.

'So kind of like me and Ryn, hey?' Sammy laughed, glancing over at Ryn who sat frozen, refusing to look at me and my apple.

'Well, yeah since we were kids. We've lived across the road from each other. Our parents were friends. I was with her when her mum died. We have kind of always just been with each other.' Sammy's hand brushed against Cobin's as they continued swinging next to each other. He definitely noticed it, he pretended he didn't, but I knew he had.

'Have you ever been more than just friends?' I nearly choked on my apple and Cobin nearly fell straight off his swing.

'Ah no, no way. Wow would that be weird. No, no way, only friends and that's how it always will be. Why? Have you and Ryn been something more?' I tried not to look at them both as they openly talked about Ryn and me, right within earshot, but I could steal little glances here and there. Sammy looked away into the distance and smiled.

* * *

I continued to sit in silence. I'd finished eating my apple and was now onto my sandwich, and Ryn was pretending to pluck out blades of grass. Why did he always look so clever and confident? What was so good about living here and being him? Well, I suppose he had a mum, so that had to help. I ripped at the crust of my sandwich and chewed roughly at it, the more I thought about Ryn the more annoyed I became.

I did wonder what he thought of me. I could probably guess, but I didn't care. I had one focus, and that was to find Skull.

* * *

Eventually I finished all of my food and I was thinking about our next step, when Cobin and Sammy jumped off the swing and returned to our conversation.

Sitting down, Sammy scruffed Cobin's hair, laughing and that was it. Definitely enough for my anger to take hold. 'Well, I'm sure glad you both could fit fun into our schedule. Now, can we get back to finding my mother's killer?' I couldn't believe they were off having fun right now. I couldn't even remember what fun felt like.

'Listen, it's getting late into the afternoon anyway. I start work tomorrow morning. Ryn and Lawlie, you can both come by then, and I can give you a pass. Cobin I guess you could come too, but it'd be easier with less people.' Sammy had all the answers, didn't she?

'Sounds like a plan. Thank you for today, I'll honestly never forget it.' Cobin sounded so meaningful when he spoke to her that I deliberately crossed my arms over my chest to avoid my clenched fists showing.

CHAPTER 9

AFTER WE HAD SAID goodbye to Sammy and Ryn for the day, Cobin and I were pretty quiet walking home along Rainbow Avenue.

'Alright, Cobin, what is going on?'

He continued to look straight ahead. 'What do you mean? With what?' He was always pretty bad at pretending.

'You and Sammy. You've been acting funny ever since we met her, all of a few hours ago, and then you both sneak off together to the swings… come on?' Cobin laughed, but still wouldn't look at me.

'We just get along really well, okay? She's fun and she's funny. I like her.' I rolled my eyes – 'fun and funny' – I didn't think she was funny at all.

'So, you mean you like her, like a lot.'

Cobin was getting frustrated, I could hear it in his voice as he said, 'I dunno Law, it's my business isn't it? What do you care?'

What did I care, really? I just didn't want their 'thing' or whatever it was about to become interfering with my plans. 'Well, don't get too friendly, we're out of here at the end of the week you know.' Cobin ignored me.

We walked into Jewel's house around dinner time and Markus was already home from his community role. He greeted us with a wide smile, not unlike Jewel's, 'Well, hello you two. Jewel has been filling me in. So great to see you both, but sorry about the circumstances. How is your dad, Cobin?' Cobin gave Markus a handshake and filled him in as best he could. Markus seemed like a nice man, polite and friendly, but still, he didn't need to know what we were really doing here, after all he was a community worker.

Jewel smiled. 'I'm going to finish dinner, but you guys go hang out. There's one spare room for whoever claims it, and the other can have the couch.' I couldn't have cared less, I wasn't sleeping much anyway, but Cobin insisted I take the bedroom.

At dinner, Cobin did most of the talking, actually catching up with his sister and discussing how to help his dad in the long term. I was thankful not to talk about Mum, so instead I just sat and listened.

'So, you both went out into the Void and were robbed on your way here?' Markus asked.

'Yeah, but well, we got our stuff back. Turns out it was this guy Ryn, do you know him Jewel?'

Jewel laughed. 'Of course I know him, he and Sammy have been friends with us forever. Both of their mothers are lovely, we sort of swap and sell stuff between us. Why would Ryn rob you?' Jewel looked confused by the thought.

'Well, he didn't know that we knew you. He thought we were just a couple out running the line. Anyway, he gave us our backpacks back.' It felt strange to be defending Ryn in any way.

'So, you've made friends with Sammy and Ryn, that's great. You know Sammy works over at the Waterboard.'

'Oh yeah, they seem nice, we'll probably hang out a bit while we're here.' I tried to change the subject, and anyway I was getting pretty tired. Glancing out the window it was dark, so I made my excuses and went off to my room for the night. Plus, I wanted to give Cobin a chance to catch up with his sister and brother-in-law without them feeling like I had to be included. I was more than happy to have some time to myself.

I had just laid down across the bed when I heard a knocking on my window. I knew it was dark outside and I wondered who would even think to come looking for me now. On closer look at the glass, I recognised who it was. Of course it was Ryn.

I opened the window and whispered angrily, 'What are you doing here? Don't you sleep?'

He looked a bit offended and motioned for me to keep my voice down. 'I found this at home and thought you could use it tomorrow.' He handed me a large empty water bottle.

'Couldn't you have waited until tomorrow? I wasn't going anywhere, except maybe to sleep.' Ryn looked disappointed by my reaction, but not all that surprised.

'I just wanted you to have it, as part of our plan. I'll go now, enjoy your sleep.'

He started to back away and I reached out and grabbed his arm. 'Look, wait, maybe I could pop out for a bit without them noticing. They'd kill me if they knew I had left at night, but maybe just for a bit.' Now that Ryn had actually come by it was a great excuse to explore this place a little more, especially at night when hardly anyone was around.

'I was hoping that you would say that. Come on, let's go.'

I climbed out my window and we headed down the street, Ryn was leading the way as I was busy looking around. I had never been outside at night. The AIRLOCKs made sure of that. In spite of the readily available air, WaterZone was even quieter at night and I wondered what people did here for fun. Were they always too busy working?

'I reckon we go have a look round the Waterboard, what do you think?' I smiled at his suggestion, that was exactly what I was thinking.

We headed up a long hill and I was walking slower than usual. I was pretty tired from the enormous day we'd had, but at the same time excited and curious about what I might find.

'So that's it over there.' We were hiding behind a small brick wall, crouched down and peeping over it.

'It doesn't look that big, but it goes back pretty far. Usually there are only a few people working the nightshift during this time. Do you want to get closer?' I nodded as I stared at the ugly brown bricked building. Even though it was dark, I assumed during the day it still remained a little spooky and weird.

There were tiny windows with drawn blinds and an old wooden door at the entrance. A sign out the front read 'Waterboard'. I tried to imagine working here every day, it looked so boring and awful.

'Let's go round the back and see if we can get in through a door or window.' I followed Ryn, assuming he did this kind of thing regularly. I really hoped Cobin was too busy with his sister to check on me. We slowly crept along the side of the building checking each tiny window as we passed it. Locked, locked, locked, ah ha! Open! Ryn looked at me, eyebrows raised and grinning. 'I'll boost you up, then you pull me in.'

I nodded. 'Okay, let's do it.'

He bent over and I climbed up on his back, using the wall for balance. I pulled myself into the old building. Looking into the room it was empty apart from a large desk in the corner and a chair, no one was in there so we were safe, for now.

I spun around and reached out the window and gripped Ryn's hands. Using all my strength, I dragged him in as he tried to climb the wall with his feet.

Pulling him through the window, he fell straight on top of me. I stared at him, shocked that our faces were so close and his body was resting on mine. I didn't say anything and neither did he, we just froze. I could feel his breath on my face and I could smell his sweat. I didn't hate it.

He pushed a strand of my hair off my face and smiled. I actually smiled back, and gripped his hand in mine. He looked around and spoke again, 'We better get going.' I frowned at his sudden change of tone and shoved him off me.

'Yeah, come on,' I replied. We both stood up and looked around. 'Might be an office or something?' He nodded in agreement as he walked over to the desk and tried to open the drawers, but they were locked.

'I wonder what's in them? What they're hiding.' I glanced around the room for anything else that we might be able to find but there seriously was nothing else. 'Come on, let's go have a look around.' I slowly opened the door and it revealed a long dark hallway. I nodded my head towards the door across from us, maybe we could get in there and have a look. I slowly opened the large brown door.

The next room was dark, but we could still make out some of the notes on the wall. There appeared to be a large whiteboard with directions, notes and numbers written across it. I had no idea what they meant, and from the look on Ryn's face, neither did he.

'Maybe it's just stuff related to the water. You know what comes in, what goes out, times, costs, whatever. It certainly doesn't look like there's anything about pollution.'

I shot him a look. 'Well they aren't exactly going to write that on a whiteboard for everyone to see, are they?' He bit his lip in silence, he knew I was right but he was just thinking aloud, and I was being mean.

'Alright, well maybe this is just a staff room or something. Come on, next one.' We left the second room and walked slowly down the dark hallway. Then Ryn froze, stood still, and I bumped straight into him. 'What?'

He glared at me. 'Shhhh!' he pressed his finger to his lips and narrowed his eyebrows. That was when I heard them. Voices. A rough, deep man's voice and a high-pitched woman's voice.

My eyes darted in all directions, where could we go? We were in plain sight in the hallway and the voices were getting louder. Ryn moved back and pushed me back into the staff room we had just left. Nervously looking around the room for somewhere to hide, I noticed a long green couch and ran with Ryn and jumped behind it just as the door opened.

'Skull, why haven't we heard anything?'

'I don't know, Tash. I added the polluted batches to the sales just as you suggested, and they were sold to AirZone, just as you had hoped, but so far I have heard nothing. No reports, nothing. Surely someone would notice people dying?'

Skull's voice sounded with authority. So it was him polluting the water.

'We know FireZone had eleven people go down and even a few from SoilZone, with five dead, although I was hoping for more.

Should we up the distribution number?' Tash asked, sounding calm and cold.

'Yes, everyone needs water, right? They will still buy it, even if they suspect we are polluting some of the batches, they'll risk it. I suggest we up the batches, even triple it?' said Skull.

Tash laughed a sinister laugh. 'Ahh, you read my mind. That is why I work with you. Yes, let's do it, start tomorrow. Room 201, the entire batch.'

As they left, Ryn and I looked at each other, our mouths wide open, shocked at what we had heard, but thrilled to have heard such a clear piece of evidence. We had just gotten incredibly lucky.

'Who's Tash?' I asked Ryn, thinking he might know. Shrugging, he frowned as if trying to remember who she might be.

'No idea. That was definitely Skull though, but Tash, unsure.'

'I guess she's working with Skull and trying to wipe out the zones, but why?'

'I'm not sure why but now we know what's happening, at least,' Ryn said slowly standing up.

'Yeah, we do. Room 201 tomorrow,' I stood up next to him and breathing heavily, angry yet unafraid, I walked towards the door.

'Come on, we gotta get back and tell the others. Tomorrow we are going to stop this and I am personally going to deal with Skull and this Tash woman.'

Ryn started walking over towards me. 'But Skull's Sceptre's right-hand man, Lawlie and Sceptre runs all of Virozone.'

I smiled at him and gripped his sweaty hand. 'Yeah, well not for long.'

CHAPTER 10

COBIN WAS WAITING FOR me when I snuck back in through my bedroom window, sitting at the end of the bed. He looked angry. 'Since when do you just sneak off without telling me, Law?'

I climbed in and sat across from him on a desk chair. 'You will seriously not believe what Ryn and I overheard tonight, Cobe.'

His eyebrows raised. 'Oh you snuck out with Ryn, did you?' I rolled my eyes, was he jealous? Not after him and Sammy, surely?

'That's irrelevant. Look we got into the Waterboard, and we heard Skull talking to some woman named Tash. They're planning on polluting a whole batch of water tomorrow in Room 201.'

Cobin nodded, listening to my every word. 'Well at least we have a clearer plan than we had this afternoon.'

'Yeah, we do. Look, we stick to our original arrangement. Ryn and I are going in tomorrow and we'll need you to help us so we can stop that batch from getting poisoned.' My plan sounded simple, but just how we would put it into action I had no idea.

'You know, if we were to somehow get rid of Skull, well that would stop the batch being polluted. I mean, if we got to him first and took him out.' Cobin was right – stop the actual source of the problem.

'Yeah, I could do that,' I said. And I believed that I could. I just needed a chance and I would take him out.

Cobin nodded and stood up. 'Alright, well it's late and I'm exhausted. I'll see you in the morning, Law. Maybe you'll dream about your new boyfriend!' Cobin was joking as he pushed me softly in my arm.

'Well you can dream about your new girlfriend, what do you think about that?' He laughed and exited out the door. I flung myself on the bed and fell asleep immediately, what a day and what a night.

* * *

Jewel was cooking some toast when I emerged from the bedroom, and as the comforting smell made its way to me, I realised I was starving. I was dressed in long black pants and my nicest grey t-shirt.

'Just in time! Toast?' Jewel was smiling as I entered the room. No one else was there and she winked at me. 'Cobin filled me in, it's a good plan. And I'm glad you guys have paired up with Ryn and Sammy. They're great kids and they know their way around WaterZone.' I sat down at the table as Jewel put the toast in front of me.

'Yeah, I hope we can pull it off,' I said, trying to sound confident. Jewel came and sat across from me, handing me the jar of strawberry jam.

'So, what can I do? Come on, I need to be more involved. How can I be useful?' I spread some jam across my toast and took a bite, thinking about how best we could use Jewel. Cobin came out and joined us, scooping out a huge tablespoon of jam as he sat down.

'Okay, so Ryn and I are going into the Waterboard today. Sammy will already be in there to let us in. I know it's a bit dramatic, but can you and Cobin cause some sort of distraction?'

Jewel thought about this for a moment and replied, 'Yeah I think I can. What time?'

I made some mental notes in my head. 'I think about 11am. That will give us time to get in, find Skull and then deal with him while you guys distract everyone else in the board.'

Cobin draped his arm around Jewel. 'Thanks again for agreeing to help us. I know how hard this must be with Markus and everything. Law, can you give us a signal or something when you're in position?'

I thought for a moment, what could I possibly do that wouldn't be too noticeable, but clear enough for Jewel and Cobin to see? I looked down at the table and spotted the empty bottle Ryn had brought me last night. 'What about I leave this on the window sill of the Waterboard in plain sight, if it's in the window you're right to go?'

Jewel nodded. 'Yep that's a good idea and then we'll begin our big distraction.'

Cobin chewed his toast loudly. 'So, what's your big plan for the distraction, sis?'

'Well, my dear brother, it just so happens that I'm in the possession of something special and I have been waiting for just the right time to use it.' Cobin's eyebrows raised.

'Alright, spill, what have you got?'

Jewel pulled out a small glass jar filled with clear liquid.

'What is that?'

She passed it to Cobin. 'Open it slowly and smell it.' Cobin, confused but intrigued, did as his sister said. As he sniffed at the old jar he grinned widely.

'This isn't what I think it is, is it?' Jewel smiled in return, she'd been saving it for a very long time.

'Actual fuel, can you believe it? Markus came across it on a run a few years ago and we had no idea what to do with it. We knew it was worth a bunch, but how do you get rid of something so rare?' She looked over at me, sitting, staring like Cobin.

'Wow. What a perfect time to use it. This will be just right.' I grabbed the jar from Cobin and shook the liquid around. Both Cobin and I had only heard about fuel in stories passed down and passed around, but to actually smell it and see it was amazing.

'You're going to set this on fire, aren't you?' Cobin added, snatching the jar back in awe.

Jewel laughed. 'Yeah, that's my grand plan. Throw it into the Waterboard alight and run like hell!' We were impressed. I knew Jewel was tough, but not this tough. She had a fair bit of guts.

Cobin put the jar on the table and got serious. 'Alright, but we need to suit up. Cover our faces, no one can know that it's us.' And just then, Markus walked in, home early from a run.

'No one can know it was you, doing what?' Markus asked, and Jewel's mouth dropped open, but no words came out. Cobin shut his mouth tightly, unsure what to say.

'Alright you three, I knew something was up last night. You had better tell me the entire story. Jewel what are you getting mixed up in?' Markus was right, we needed to tell him the truth and maybe, just maybe we could actually use his help, or maybe he would dob us in and we'd be evaporated.

I took the lead, after all, it was my idea. I filled him in. When

I was finished, the four of us sat in silence in the kitchen. Jewel sat still, biting her lip.

Markus scratched his head. 'Looks like we better get moving. It'll be 11am pretty soon and I'm sure another pair of hands wouldn't go astray.' Jewel ran over to him and hugged him, almost tipping him straight off his chair. Cobin and I stopped holding our breath and realised we could breathe again.

* * *

Cobin was the first to stand up. 'Well we better get over to Ryn's and get going, I'm sure you're happy about that, Law.' Okay that was it, I had had enough of his annoying comments.

'Oh get over it Cobin. I know you think you're funny but you're annoying and I think you're trying to cover for the fact that you're madly, head over heels in love with our new-found friend, Sammy.'

Cobin's face went bright red and he looked over at his sister awkwardly, Jewel had the widest grin across her face but didn't utter a word. 'Let's go, Law,' was all he said, picking up his backpack and leaving out the door. I followed, after a quick smirk at Jewel.

Not letting her baby brother get away with a thing, Jewel yelled out behind us, 'Say hi to Sammy for me Cobin won't you?' I burst out laughing but Cobin continued on in front, refusing to turn around and refusing to carry this on any further.

As we arrived at Ryn's we found him already outside leaning against his front fence, leg crossed and silently waiting. 'Was wondering where you two were. Come on, we gotta get going.' I didn't think we were late and I wondered why he was suddenly quite serious and abrupt.

I tried to lighten the mood with an off-handed comment, 'Sorry, ah Cobin was just day-dreaming about Sammy.' I laughed but no one else did. Cobin stormed off in front and Ryn refused to comment. What was with these guys?

I followed Ryn and grabbed his elbow. 'What's wrong? Is everything alright?' I was serious, because I was seriously worried something was up and we couldn't pull this off if he was ignoring me.

He stopped and turned towards me. 'No everything's fine, Lawlie. I just think we need to take this more seriously. We are actually trying to stop this large new batch of water getting polluted and in doing so, possibly kill a man. Sorry if I don't feel like joking around.'

I screwed up my face, what did he mean he was going to kill a man? I was responsible for this and I was deadly serious about it.

'Hey, you know I can do it, don't you? I only need you to get me in there, that's all, end of the road for you. I'll stop the poison, I'll take out Skull and Tash and Sceptre if he's there too.' I sounded tough because I was and I didn't need anyone's help, I had enough anger inside of me to take out the whole Waterboard if I had to.

'You say that now, Lawlie, but have you ever actually killed someone before?'

I took a step back. 'Well, no, but I will. Don't question me Ryn. You didn't see my mother, you weren't there.' I gritted my teeth, determined not to cry, but I could feel the tears streaming down my face in spite of myself. Ryn looked at me sadly and pulled me in for a warm hug.

Brushing my hair with his hand he hugged me even tighter and whispered, 'We just need to be careful. Skull might not be the only one dying today, that scares me, Lawlie.' I suppose I hadn't thought of that, just as easy as I could take out Skull, he could take out any one of us.

Just then, Cobin's familiar voice interrupted us, 'Alright you two, come on. Sammy said this morning. I'm heading back to help Jewel. Can you handle this?'

I pulled away slowly from Ryn and looked up into his green eyes, yeah, we could do this.

'Alright, let's go.'

After a quick hug from Cobin and a slightly awkward handshake between Cobin and Ryn we got moving, and fast. Just like last night we could see the Waterboard from a distance, big and ugly.

It looked different to last night, there was a small counter at the opening of the Waterboard and I could see the window where we would place the bottle. Standing next to the window was Sammy, running her hand through her long hair a little too quickly.

'Well hello, Ryn,' Sammy smiled, greeting us as she would anyone coming to get some water.

'Hey, Sammy. Lawlie and I are here to collect some water, can you show us around?' Sammy smiled and placed two orange wristbands around our wrists.

To anyone who was watching, we all appeared legitimate. Just two people, looking for water.

'Come through this way and I'll show you in.' Sammy led us both into a long hallway, different to the one we snuck into last night.

I looked at her closely and her smile widened as we passed a couple of elderly factory workers. She pulled me in closely for a hug and whispered quickly in my ear, 'Room 45. Get there, and we can talk.'

I smiled back. 'Thank you.'

I stepped out of her hug as she spoke to the both of us again. 'Now, if you head up that way, towards the end of the hallway on your left you'll find Room 10 and that's one of the stock rooms.' Ryn and I nodded as she continued, 'Now I have to head out the front again quickly, but I'll find you again soon, okay.'

'No wait!' I could have kicked myself. The water bottle, the one I was supposed to bring to put in the window sill, it was back at Jewel's.

'I forgot the water bottle for the signal. I–' I was trying to explain it when suddenly a deep voice interrupted from behind.

'Here, take this. Do what you need to do.' We all spun around, someone had overheard us, now someone knows our plan.

'You!' I couldn't believe who it was, the man from the Void, who I gave free water to. He was here and he didn't look all that desperate at all.

'Think of this as repaying the favour.' He smiled and winked as I accepted the water bottle from his thick hand.

'I, thanks.' I managed to get out as he nodded and ran. He knew what we were here to do and he obviously wanted no part of it.

I could tell Sammy and Ryn were confused, but I'd fill them in later. Right now I handed the empty bottle to Sammy.

'Can you place this on the front window sill at 11am? It's Cobin and Jewel's signal for the distraction.' She took the bottle I handed her and nodded.

We thanked her and I leaned into Ryn. '45 – we gotta get to Room 45.' He nodded and led me left down to the next adjoining hallway. Travelling down the hall, we saw a few workers here and there, but no one gave us a second glance with our wrist bands on. Most didn't smile or even look at us, they just kept their eyes straight ahead, moving almost mindlessly.

Room 45 was empty except for a few empty canister crates in the corner. Sammy came in minutes later and quietly closed the door behind her.

'This is pretty much one of the only rooms that I know is free. No one will hear or see us.' Sammy grabbed a couple of crates and motioned for us to sit down. Sitting in a semi-circle we filled her in on our adventure last night.

'So, we came here last night,' Ryn began as Sammy's eyes widened. 'You did what?'

I could tell she was worried, so I jumped in, 'Look we had to suss it out to see what was going on and we overheard Skull and some lady called Tash. They are going to ruin all the batches.'

Sammy breathed out loudly. 'Wow. Okay, so how do we stop this?'

I smiled at Ryn who was smiling back as I stood up. 'With your help!'

Sammy went through the directions to Room 201 and explained that if we took a left out of this room, and climbed two flights of stairs, Room 201 was immediately to our left. Ryn and I both listened intently as she described what the water purifying room looked like.

'So, it's a huge room, heaps of canisters, probably a funnel leading to a section of the well. But in saying that, all you really need is to get to Skull before he puts the pollution in, get rid of him and then we alert the zone to what is going on.'

As if reading her mind, Ryn interrupted, 'Once we alert the zone, hopefully there will be some sort of uprising. Maybe they'll even storm the Waterboard.' I wasn't sure what would happen, but

I knew we had about ten minutes until 11am and we had to get moving. After all, we had Skull to kill and zones to save.

CHAPTER 11

I **LOOKED OUT THE** window of our room and I could see Cobin, Markus and Jewel hiding way, way back behind a half-broken brick wall. I knew they could see the Waterboard from their position, it was perfect for all three of them to fit behind without being seen.

'Go now Sammy and put it on the sill, they're in place and will act on your signal.' Sammy nodded and locked eyes with me. I could almost read her mind. She was scared but she was also brave.

'You got this, Sam,' Ryn said, grabbing her arm for support and she smiled, her perfect, beautiful smile.

'Of course I do. Now you two do your job and get to Room 201.'

With that, she spun around and left, heading quickly to her position in the front of the Waterboard. Ryn and I stood in silence staring at each other, waiting for the exact moment we would bolt to Room 201. And then we heard her, it was Sammy and she was screaming.

'Fire! We have a fire! Evacuate, now!' Sammy was yelling at the top of her voice.

We didn't have time to think we just ran, following Sammy's directions as best we could. We could smell the smoke and feel some of the heat, but we couldn't stop.

The flames started to move throughout the building. It was an old building with old furniture, made from old materials and of course, old wood. Everything was just so old! The flames shot down the hallway like a red-hot trail.

Workers from inside the Waterboard came barreling out the front door, shocked and choking on the smoke. Confused by what was happening they yelled at each other for answers.

'What is happening in there!?'

'Is it an attack!?'

'Maybe something exploded?'

I could hear their voices in the distance, but I didn't stop, neither of us stopped, we ran to Room 201.

CHAPTER 12

WE EVENTUALLY MADE OUR way to the outside of Room 201. No one stopped us, and I was pretty sure everyone had evacuated, so we made it there quickly. Ryn and I stood there for about half a minute, looking at each other and the door, wondering what exactly we would find behind it and if we could really go ahead with our plan.

A banging roared overhead. It sounded loud and clear just as I had my hand on the door handle. I pulled back in shock before I realised what it was. A voice suddenly yelled through the speakers: 'Leave the building. This is not a drill. Leave the building.' The loud robotic voice repeated over and over, I had to ignore it and put my hand on the doorknob. Ryn placed his hand safely over mine and we breathed deeply as our hands twisted the handle and pushed open the door together.

Pushing open the door, we saw exactly who I expected to see. Someone large with short dark combed-over hair and a tattooed dark face in the shape of a skull. Yep, there was no mistaking him, it was Skull.

'Stop right now, Skull, we know what you're doing,' I yelled at him as he stared at us, two water bottles in his ugly hands.

He straightened up and frowned. 'And who are you?'

'Me.' I kicked him in the shin as hard as I could.

He came crashing down to the ground, grabbing at his leg and yelling as he hit the floor hard. I jumped back just as Ryn knocked him out with a quick hard punch to his head.

So Skull wasn't that tough after all.

'We gotta drag him. Come on, you get his arms, I've got his legs.' Skull had passed out, but we didn't know for how long, so we had to act. I looked around the room for somewhere to put him, he was heavy so we couldn't move him far.

'The cupboard over there, let's chuck him in there and close the door. We could shove some chairs or something up against it to try to lock him in.'

Dragging him into the cupboard, we slammed the door and looked around the room for stuff to block it and hold it closed. We were in luck! There were a couple of old chairs and a heavy table, which we managed to skid across the room.

'I don't know if this will hold. What if he gets out and attacks us?' Ryn looked around for a weapon and came across a broom. 'I can use this.' He banged the old broom on the floor. I laughed, but only for a second. We needed something better than a broom.

Scanning the room, I realised that Sammy was right, it was full of water bottles and knobs and a long hose on the left-hand side that I could only assume led down into the water supply. Maybe that was where Skull was going to tip in his pollution.

My exploration was halted by his muffled voice coming from the cupboard, Skull was starting to wake up and I needed some answers.

'What are you doing here with the water supply?' I demanded, giving the cupboard door a kick.

'Hey! I wouldn't do that again if I was you, little girl,' he sounded angry and I imagined his tattooed face screwed up in hatred towards us.

'We're here for you. Have you tipped in the pollution yet? Have you ruined the batch?' Skull laughed or growled, I couldn't tell which.

'How do you know about that? Well, so what. You're too late, I tipped it in ages ago.' He was clearly enjoying the fact that we were too late to stop him.

I looked across at Ryn who shrugged and banged the door with his fist. Then I spotted it.

'No, he's lying, the liquid is there. We're not too late, Ryn!' Hope rose tentatively through me.

'Believe what you will, little girl, but you'll have no chance to escape. Soon Sceptre will be here.' Was he bluffing?

'Why do this anyway? Huh, what do you gain from it?' I wanted him to own up and spill his story and he did.

'Well don't you see that if we kill off everyone in all of your pathetic zones that the PreZone prevails? We can move our Prestige communities in there and we can flourish. We don't need you lot anymore. We can start again with actual civilised people. Every zone can be a PreZone!' I couldn't believe his arrogance, how could he possibly think he could just kill off all of us?

'That is one crazy idea you have there.' I screwed up my face, rolling my eyes at Ryn, mocking Skull for his ridiculous ideas.

'Not that crazy. Not crazy if you're Sceptre,' he replied.

He was serious. Completely serious, and he was actually in with a chance of succeeding here. Especially if he had already shipped the polluted water to each of the zones. But where was this Tash from last night?

'So, what now?' I asked Ryn quietly. But he just looked back at me and shrugged. Great. We both had absolutely no clue what we should do, meanwhile Skull began banging against the door, and he was strong.

Suddenly, Sammy burst into Room 201, breathing fast and sweating as if she'd just ran both flights of stairs.

She surveyed the room, speechless for a moment. 'I can't believe you did it,' she finally managed.

I looked at her, somewhat disappointed, and replied, 'Well, we think we stopped the polluted batches being sent out, but we can't be positive.'

Sammy squinted her eyes and walked over to the cupboard door and put her face close.

'Alright, Skull, here's how this is going to go. You're going to tell me the truth or I will do something far more sinister than you can ever imagine.'

Skull laughed. 'Oh really, what do you think you can do to me?' he yelled back.

Sammy grinned. 'We'll tie you up and take you out into the Void, just as you are now and we'll leave you there. I can't imagine you would last too long. We'll give you a BA, maybe. But really I don't think that will last either. You know what the Desperate are like out there, don't you?' Skull was silent, everyone knew what would happen, especially if you were someone as prominent as Skull.

'I don't believe you,' he said, but his quivering voice told a different story.

'I don't much care what you believe. And unless you haven't noticed, the evacuation alarm has taken care of anyone who might have realised your little situation. You two, grab that trolley.' Sammy pointed to a large wire trolley on wheels, perfect for transporting Skull.

'Alright, alright! I haven't polluted the water yet.' I looked at Ryn and Sammy and nodded, relieved that we had stopped him from poisoning this batch, but what about the next? Or the one after that?

'I'm going to evaporate you Skull, just as you killed my mother. I'm going to destroy you!' I yelled through the wooden door, as both Ryn and Sammy helped hold it shut against him.

'Good luck little girl. Sceptre is on his way if he's not here already and then you are all evaporated.'

Ryn grabbed my arm. 'He's right, this whole thing has taken way too long. The alarms sounded ages ago. We gotta go and we gotta go *now!*'

My eyes stayed fixated on the cupboard, there was no way I could leave without getting my revenge on Skull.

'Lawlie, Ryn's right, we need to leave. And the smoke, can't you smell it? We'll be dead ourselves.' Sammy was worried as I followed her eyes around the room.

She was right, grey smoke had begun filling the room, creeping in under the door like a ghost. I banged my fists hard against the door, they were right, we had to go.

'This hasn't finished, Skull, you're as good as evaporated. I'm not done with you!' I screamed with every last bit of hatred I could find locked away deep inside. I felt Sammy and Ryn pulling me away by my arms, through the haunting smoke as it took over the room and we ran.

We bolted out of Room 201 together and linking arms we entered the hallway. It was smoky and I could hardly breathe, hating myself for leaving Skull, but I knew I needed to leave, and leave with my friends.

CHAPTER 13

WE BOLTED DOWN THE first flight of stairs, but lost our grip on each other. I thought we had all made it to the second stairs, but I could barely see through the smoke. I came down the second flight, coughing and choking. I could see Ryn, he was next to me the entire time. I felt his body close to mine as we squeezed out the front door we had come in earlier.

'Are you okay?' I asked as we collapsed out the front of the burning building. He gave me a quick thumbs up and fell to his knees. Just as he fell, his head shot up frantically.

'Where's Sammy?' His voice was desperate as he looked over at the burning building.

'I dunno. I thought sh—we must have been separated. Maybe she got out another way?' I was trying to sound hopeful.

'Could someone have grabbed her?' I could tell Ryn was thinking the same thing.

'I've gotta go back in.' Ryn was trying to stand up, but collapsed again in a fit of coughing. I was suddenly aware of the onlookers and knew we had to disappear before people started asking questions about us.

'No, we've got to go, Ryn, people are staring. We have to leave now.' He looked around at the factory workers as they stared at us. It wouldn't be long before Sceptre's armed security started rounding up and interviewing suspects.

'But I can't leave her! She could be trapped in there. If it was Cobin, Lawlie, what would you do?' I knew he was right, but if we were caught, we were dead.

I dragged Ryn behind the broken stone wall. A few factory workers saw us, but it didn't look as if they cared too much.

'What if she doesn't come out, Ryn?' I peered over the wall at the burning building, the fire was slowly becoming under control.

'She has to. She just has to,' Ryn said through clenched teeth. I wondered where she could have gone, how we lost her and then I saw them. Skull held Sammy by her arms as she tried to pull out of his grip. I didn't know what he was saying but she was yelling as Skull pulled her along, twisting her arm. He was quick to try and bypass the crowd and the curious eyes of the factory workers. Ryn and I stopped far enough back from them so we couldn't be seen. 'Where's that rat taking her?' Ryn asked.

'We should go see, come on.' I grabbed his arm as we began to sneak through the crowd to the left-hand side of the Waterboard.

Ryn and I watched as Skull led her over to his motorbike.

'What is he going to do? Take her with him?' I asked, confused and even more angry at myself for allowing Skull to escape.

Ryn was frozen next to me, staring at Skull holding Sammy by her wrist.

'He's going to evaporate her. He's trying to remove her I.D. Brace!' Ryn pushed past me as he ran at Skull as Sammy struggled to get her wrist free from his grasp.

I chased Ryn, this could not be happening. But it was.

'Sammy!' Ryn screamed, accidently distracting Sammy from breaking loose and allowing a microsecond of time for Skull to rip off her I.D. Brace. She smiled at Ryn and then she went limp.

Skull threw Sammy to the ground and climbed on his big black motorcycle. Grinning at both Ryn and me, he kick-started the bike and rode away from the remaining flames that were engulfing the Waterboard. Waterboard workers were still trying to put them out, but I could tell Ryn had only one thing on his mind.

We both squatted down next to her, she was evaporating slowly and would soon dissolve into nothing, so she didn't have much time.

'Sammy! I–' Ryn didn't know what to say as Sammy laid on her back.

'It's okay, Lawlie, you need to take this.' I frowned, what was she talking about? I followed her half-closed eyes as she looked down at her closed fist. Her WaterZone I.D. Brace was gone, why would I need that?

'What? I don't understand?' I said. Maybe she was confused, disorientated?

'Yes, you do. This, you need this.' With her last effort of strength she slowly opened her hand to reveal what she was clutching so tightly – a second I.D. Brace. And not just any I.D. Brace, but a PreZone I.D. Brace.

'What?' Both Ryn and I stared in shock, how had Ryn not known that Sammy was from the PreZone?

I could tell he had a million questions to ask her, but no sound escaped his mouth.

'Go there, Lawlie, find my brother,' she whispered breathlessly as she slipped the PreZone I.D. Brace into my hand. The four zone colours of the Brace shone brightly in my palm. I pressed my face closer to hers, gripping her shoulders and begging her to stay awake.

'But, who's your brother, who is he?' I asked, desperately wanting some answers.

She smiled, her beautiful smile and squeezed my arm softly. 'Chance. Chance Radcliff. Sceptre's son and heir to Virozone.'

CHAPTER 14

We didn't hang around long at the charred Waterboard. Some of WaterZone townsfolk had put out the flames and it was half standing, half smouldering. No one looked at us.

We got back to Jewel's faster than usual, we needed to get moving and fast. Cobin ran at me as soon as he saw me enter the house. I had no idea how I looked, but I assumed it was fairly bad.

'You okay?' He hugged me so tightly and I started to cough again. Ryn sat down at the kitchen table with Jewel and Markus. It took Cobin a moment to realise it was only Ryn and me, and that Sammy was missing.

'Where's Sammy?' he asked anxiously. Yep I was pretty sure he'd been in love with her.

'She got caught, Cobin. Skull evaporated her.' Jewel gasped and Cobin looked confused.

'What do you mean? How did she get caught? Why didn't you three stick together?' I put my arm around his waist and pulled him in close.

'Cobin, it was smoky and we got busted, we lost her, okay.' I continued to fill them in with what we knew. 'Skull is Sceptre's lackey. He works for him and he's the one who polluted the water.

We just stopped him from sending another huge batch to the other zones to kill who knows how many innocent people.'

Markus interrupted, 'Well what can we do now? Should I contact the WaterZone community leader? Maybe they could do something, although it seems hopeless.' Everyone looked at each other.

Then I spoke, 'Well, not that hopeless. I do have this,' and reaching into my pocket I pulled out the PreZone female I.D. Brace. I explained how Sammy had owned this all along and how she told me to find Chance Radcliff, the Prestige, Sceptre's son... her brother? No one said anything.

Cobin was the first to speak, 'You should go to PreZone Law and find Chance.'

Ryn interrupted, 'No you should not go. You'll die just like Sammy!'

Cobin spoke again, 'No one else can go and hundreds more will die if Lawlie doesn't.'

Ryn stood up from his seat and approached Cobin. 'She is not going.'

What was this turning into? No one tells me what I can and can't do.

I stood up pushing the table out roughly. 'Well, I am going and you two can sit around here and fight it out but I am going. Right now.'

Finally Ryn realised who he was dealing with and began to see some sense. 'Well, you can't go on your own. Take Markus and Jewel.'

I rolled my eyes, why did he think I needed anyone to come? They couldn't anyway they didn't have the PreZone I.D. Brace. 'They can't go. They have work to do here. They still need to eat, trade and someone needs to tell Sammy's mother what's going on. Anyway they don't have the I.D. Brace, I do. No, I'll go on my own, I'll be fine.'

I didn't know if I'd be fine or not, but I certainly didn't need a chaperone.

'Well, just promise me you'll be careful out there,' was all Ryn could say as he looked sad, remembering Sammy.

But rather than cry or sulk, I shoved some supplies into my backpack and stared at him, directly in his green eyes. 'Let's just get one thing straight here,' I said scowling, 'If you think I'm careful about anything I ever do, you don't know me at all.' And with that I stormed out the door.

CHAPTER 15

'HEY, LAW, WAIT UP, don't leave like this.' Cobin chased me out the front door. I could have guessed he would be the one to come after me.

'What? Shouldn't you be in there grieving with your old mate, Ryn?' I was walking fast, wanting to get to the exit as fast as possible and leave WaterZone permanently. I needed to get into PreZone and I needed to go there *now*.

'Hey! Can you just stop?' Cobin grabbed my arm to slow me down and I begrudgingly stopped and spun around to face him.

'What? What do you want from me?'

Cobin looked hurt and confused, he paused and began, 'I was hoping you'd let me come with you. We're still friends you know.' I put my hands on my hips and sighed.

I knew he was right. It'd only been two days, but everything had changed. I looked back at Jewel's house with my hands still firmly stuck on my hips.

'I can deal with it myself, Cobin. I've got to save innocent people who will die in all the zones if I don't get there in time and stop Sceptre, so I've got a few things on my mind.' And with that I stalked off once again. I didn't expect him to chase me this time and he didn't, so I didn't even bother to look back.

I continued to walk along the footpath, past houses and driveways that all looked the same, as I began to reflect on all the craziness of the past week.

I walked past another house and a few WaterZone residents were talking but they stopped abruptly as I went past. I glared at them, what were they talking about that was so important? I was on a serious life or death mission and I certainly didn't have any time for their problems.

I continued on and for some reason my father came into my mind. What if he lived in PreZone? What if it was there he moved to all those years ago? What if he's living with a new family and I find him? I just had to find him.

I touched my silver necklace again and promised myself that one day I would find my father, whoever he was.

I could see the exit to WaterZone up ahead and began to undo my BA from the bag. I didn't need to show any pass to leave, so I walked straight up to a short stumpy man at the gate. He didn't smile just stared at me and moved his eyes towards the exit, as if that could get me to leave his precious zone more quickly. I was about to cross the boundary line, leading out into the Void when I found myself breathing hard and fast.

Calm down, you can do this. You'll go straight to PreZone. I knew I was fit and I could run most of the way. I looked down at my feet and willed them to move, and eventually they did only to be stopped, dead in their tracks.

'Hey, you're not leaving without us, are you?' I spun around it was Ryn and Cobin.

'Don't you have anything to say? You usually have everything to say.' It was Ryn, baiting me again.

'Well, you know I don't need your help. I was prepared to go on my own. You can't even get into PreZone, only I can.' I sounded mean, because I had to be. I needed to be tough.

'Well, we'll get you there, we'll go together. Three is better than one out in the Void, even you must know that.' Cobin smiled and Ryn stuck out his hand.

'Friends?' he asked. I rolled my eyes.

'You can just put your hand back in your pocket there mate, and if you want to follow me then you can, I suppose I can't stop you.'

They looked at each other and burst out laughing. I looked from Cobin to Ryn and smiled, but only just a little smile as I pulled my BA on and started walking towards PreZone.

CHAPTER 16

'HEY, LAWLIE, YOU KNOW there's a bus from WaterZone to PreZone, don't you?' I stopped as Ryn yelled out.

'What?' I spun around and saw both of them with huge grins on their boyish faces.

'A bus. You can just catch the work bus. Everyone who works in PreZone is bussed back and forth every day from WaterZone. So you could probably just jump on that.' Ryn laughed and Cobin joined in.

'Well you might have mentioned that before we all ended up out here. Now, where is this bus?'

* * *

I stood back in Jewel's kitchen, closely inspecting the PreZone I.D. Brace. Although there were clear differences in the colours, all I.D. Braces had the same two buttons; one identity information, the second, evaporation. I had too many questions and really no way at this moment of finding any answers. I could hear Cobin and Ryn eating breakfast in the next room, chatting with Jewel. I wore my usual clothes, but tried to pick the best from a bad lot, knowing I would transform into PreZone attire when I put on the I.D. Brace. I had been saving my money for about a year, hoping to purchase a new bike, since my last one ended up mangled in Death Creek. I had exactly thirty-seven mirc which would allow for food and cheap accommodation in the PreZone, for at least a couple of days anyway. All zones traded in the same currency, which this time worked out well. The Prestige loved to exploit us and take our money whenever they could; I guess that they think it's easier if we all have the same currency.

'Hey, you've really dressed up today, Lawlie.' Cobin noticed as I walked into the lounge room. He was serious as he looked me up and down. I had traded my old, ripped jeans for my newer ripped jeans and my usual grey t-shirt was replaced with a dark green shirt, faded red jacket and sneakers. I'd brushed my hair and pulled it back into a low ponytail. I suppose I didn't look so bad for AirZone standards, but I knew I had a long way to go to impress the PreZone clones and hoped the I.D. Brace would work.

I took a sip of water and sat down at the table where Cobin and Ryn were talking.

Ryn's eyebrows rose as he looked at me, grinning. 'Oh, are you sure you're not dressing up to impress Chance, then?'

I almost spat out my water. 'No, I can guarantee you it's not to impress Chance.'

Cobin chimed in, right on inappropriate cue, 'Yeah, that's why you look different. To impress Chance Radcliff.' I kicked him hard under the table. 'Aw!' he yelped.

'Just knock it off, you two. What, are you jealous that I'll be hanging out with someone else, someone in the Prestige, and not you?!'

Cobin smiled. 'No, Lawlie, you look nice, really nice.'

I screwed up my face. 'Yeah, I guess.' I didn't want to get into anything with those two about Chance. I had a job to do, a job I didn't ask to do, but one that must be done. We didn't need to spend the morning teasing each other. After all, this could be the last time I saw them if something bad was to happen to me in PreZone. But I didn't want to think about that.

* * *

'Well, are we going to do this, or what?' I was impatient, I still wanted my revenge on Skull.

The boys stood up and Jewel reached over and grabbed my hand. 'You be careful.' She was serious and I knew she was thinking about Sammy, we all were.

With my backpack full to the top with clothes, I nodded and walked out the front door, Ryn and Cobin following close behind. Even though I didn't know where I was going, I was sure Ryn would point us in the right direction. It took about ten minutes for us to walk straight to Marley's Bakehouse. The Bakehouse was a small rundown bakery, which was cheap enough, but more importantly, was the exact location of the bus stop, which headed straight to the PreZone.

Standing around waiting for the bus Ryn coughed nervously and spoke, 'Hey, I thought you might like to know that the Prestige are having a party tomorrow tonight in their PreZone, an actual, old style, classic ball, in a ballroom, a masquerade ball.'

I raised my eyebrows. 'Really, and how do you know?' Ryn laughed and glanced at Cobin, who also smiled, as if they had some sort of in joke, and the joke apparently was me.

'Well, I read the newspapers, Lawlie, and there was a huge double page advertisement about it. You know what PreZoners are like, anything to show off to us.'

I had to agree, they did love to flaunt their wealth, parties and social agenda in front of us whenever they could. Compared to our discos in the hall back in AirZone, which could only be run from 4pm until 5.30pm due to AIRLOCK curfew, they certainly led far more interesting lives than we could ever imagine. But of course they could with unlimited resources.

'Well, I'll have to go, won't I? I mean, I don't know what I'll wear or how I'll get in, but I have to be there right?' Was I convincing myself more than Cobin and Ryn? Inside I seriously had my doubts about even getting into PreZone, let alone attending a Prestige event.

'Just don't be yourself, Lawlie and you'll be fine.' I honestly thought Cobin expected me to fail, well get busted at least. But I didn't care, I had to find Chance. Then, at that exact second, the large black PreZone bus arrived. The driver, a large burly man, got out and entered Marley's Bakehouse for his morning tea. With his neatly pressed pants and tight-fitting blue buttoned up shirt, he looked clean and relaxed, like all PreZoners I suppose.

We all watched him enter the Bakehouse and I knew it was my chance to make my move into the storage unit underneath the bus. We ran over, Cobin held open the long rectangle door and I gave him a quick hug and I whispered, 'I'll be okay, Spare.' I pulled away as Cobin smiled and I grabbed Ryn in a quick embrace, unsure if he felt left out, and because I kind of wanted to hug him, too. But at that moment he turned his head and brushed his face across, his lips touching mine, and he kissed me slowly and sweetly. A wave of heat fuelled my body, like a rush of fire, and I could feel my face heating up like a furnace. We both pulled away. Embarrassed, I jumped in the storage unit and ran down the back and hid behind two large boxes, not looking back or saying a word, and definitely not wanting to know what Cobin thought.

I heard the storage door slam shut and I was in total darkness, though I was probably glowing bright red with embarrassment and something else... what was it? A sort of lightheaded feeling, flushing throughout my body. Whatever that feeling was, it would certainly stay with me for a long, long time, or at least for the rest of the bus ride anyway.

It didn't take long for the driver to get back on the bus and I could hear voices, older ladies getting onto the bus. I couldn't recognise anyone's voice, they were too muffled.

With the loud engine roaring to a start, I balanced myself as best I could between the back wall of the bus and the two boxes concealing me from view. I patted my pocket, and felt the I.D. Brace, yep, I was really doing this. I couldn't believe how people could travel to and from work to serve the privileged, rich Prestige in PreZone.

The boxes slid as the bus veered around corners, but I held onto them as best I could, trying not to make more noise than necessary. Then we stopped. I looked at my watch. Why had we stopped? I sank down lower behind the boxes, my eyes darting from side to side and my fists clenched tight.

I heard a loud angry voice. 'Work I.D. Braces out, WaterZone scum, hurry up, get em out, or we'll shoot ya.' The angry voice was snickering, an evil, angry laugh, muffled through a mask. It was the voice of a Captor. His friends I assumed were sniggering also, cheering him on.

'Yeah hurry up, WaterZone rats, get 'em out, can't take any chances letting you scum into our zone, you need to prove you work there.'

Was this usual? Or was it a surprise raid? Most of all, what the hell was I going to do if they decided to check in the storage compartment?

I heard the first Captor growl again, 'Now open up that door, gotta check you ain't got any stowaways trying to sneak into our zone now, don't we?'

I imagined them in their haunting gas masks, like the ones I see outside my window during AIRLOCK and I shivered. What would they look like up close? Terrifying. I looked around desperately, that's it, goodbye everyone, death sentence here I come. There was nowhere to hide, they'd pull out the two boxes and find me, search me, assume I stole the I.D. Brace and kill me.

That's it! The I.D. Brace!

I didn't know what else to do, so I pulled it out of my pocket and clasped it over my wrist. Immediately my appearance transformed. Not totally, I was still me, but my brown hair came out of the ponytail and became longer, shinier and glossier. My teeth became perfectly white, my green eyes, glistened and glowed. Even my skin felt softer. I looked at myself in the reflection of the shiny bus wall and couldn't believe who was staring back at me. Even my clothes became cleaner, brighter, rip-free and you could quite easily tell I was meant for the PreZone.

The storage door lifted up and light hit me in the face, and I became my new character almost immediately. 'Close that lid would you, you rude people.' The driver stared at me wide eyed. The Captors, who were holding evaporation guns pointed straight at me, narrowed their eyes through their clear plastic masks suspiciously. I couldn't help but almost gasp at their appearance, they were more frightening in person. There were three of them, they usually travelled in threes and each had matching clear masks, monster-like in appearance. They were in all black and even in the daylight they scared me. But I had to put on a show, after all I was now from the PreZone. 'Do you mind? I'm trying to get home and there is no way I was going to sit up there with those WaterZone rats.'

'Oh, we're sorry miss, didn't realise. Could you ah, show us your I.D. Brace, just to make sure, you know, that you are legit.' I pretended to look insulted.

'You arrogant man, here, look if you like,' and I shoved my wrist in his face. He looked at it closely, his eyes narrowed through his mask and he nodded his ugly, fat head.

'Very sorry ma'am, not usual for a Prestige to be traveling in storage, you should be up the top and make all these scum travel underneath.'

I paused. 'Ha, I agree, but you know sometimes I like to live a little, experience life from all angles, goodness knows I never get to do anything scary or rash in the PreZone. This is kind of a little adventure for me, slumming it.' I snorted, trying to mimic their evil noise from before, and they cackled too, as if they understood exactly what I meant.

'Well miss, you're welcome to stay down here, if that's what you want. Sorry to hold you up, gotta check all the worker's I.D.'s so no filth get in. You know how it is.'

I snickered, 'I certainly do, I would hate for anyone to try and sneak in to the PreZone uninvited.' I moved back under into my position behind the boxes and one of the Captors gave me a blanket. I took it and tried not to look at them too closely, as the bus continued on its way. I tried to think of how lucky I was to get myself out of that situation with the Captors and made a mental note to remind Cobin and Ryn just how smart I was. The bus eventually came to a stop. The air smelt different, the sounds were different and I sensed I was amongst something new, a Prestige Zone. Stepping out from the storage unit I was greeted again with bright sunlight, even brighter than before. Covering my eyes, I squinted as I became accustomed to the new environment. I threw my backpack over my shoulders and glanced up at the enormous sign above my head: 'Welcome to the PreZone, where we *are* better.' I smirked to myself, and rolled my eyes.

Ha, not for long, I thought.

CHAPTER 17

I DECIDED TO INVESTIGATE the city central before I made any accommodation plans. I couldn't believe what I was seeing. The most amazing, gorgeous people were walking up and down the main street. With their long hair, short hair, styled hair, hairclips of all different colours and silky smooth curls I almost literally stopped and stared. One woman had bright fiery red flowing locks and a man had short cut, straight moulded hair, both were almost plastic in appearance. Their clothes were elastic, slim fitting and suave. They were dressed in all colours, shapes and smooth textures. The fabric appeared flat and light, not like our dark toned, ripped jeans and grey materials. Their bodies were athletic and slender, no one I could tell was overweight, or sick looking, or pale. Their skin was glowing, a light sun kissed glow and not a freckle to be seen. Who were these people?

As if the people weren't enough to shock me, the buildings were exact square boxes, each a different, bright colour, with clear, easily identifiable writing on each. I had never imagined a place, where even the buildings were perfect. Glancing in a shop window, I saw tiny cakes with multi-coloured icing and beautiful lollies decorated on top. My eyes were wide, these were definitely not like the muffins Mum used to make back in AirZone before she was killed.

Cars sped past, but they were silent, shiny and smooth. Each driver wore black sunglasses, slick. There were no exhaust fumes or smog, the air, fresh and long lasting was clean. I took a deep breath and tried to imagine my life here, it would be perfect, and we would all be perfect.

I peered further down the street. Men and women were sipping what I assumed to be coffee on the main street, completely oblivious to the problems we faced in AirZone. They didn't have to be home by 6pm. They didn't have to rush home when random AIRLOCKs were initiated. No, they could sip their coffee in peace and go about their carefree existence, for the air was theirs forever.

I tried not to stare for too long, I didn't want to look out of place, but I couldn't help but watch these most fantastic people walk straight past me, and even more bizarre, they smiled at me! I received a smile from a woman with a short, jagged pixie cut and oceanic blue eyes. *Why would she smile at me?* I thought. Then I realised as I strode past a shop front, titled 'Lovely Locks', and I caught a glimpse of myself. I looked just like them with my impeccable hair and flawless eyes and teeth, everything was perfect really.

I didn't look like me. Well, I was me, a picture- perfect version of me. Cleaner, prettier, shinier. My jeans fit perfectly and were rip-free, my old red jacket had become plastic and bright, the latest fashion in PreZone, or so I had heard. My sneakers, white and spotless, with matching shoelaces, were brand new. I could do nothing but analyse myself in 'Lovely Locks' window, I recognised me, but didn't at the same time. I guess I had never been into make-up and dresses, none of us were in AirZone. We simply couldn't afford to like those things anyway, as we could never have them. But here, here in this Prestige Zone, I was transformed and I hoped I wouldn't get too attached to the new me. I certainly couldn't stay here forever.

As I began to walk along the main street, I wished I had packed food. Although my food at home was nothing like the magnificent delicacies here, I was famished and would settle for anything, even Mum's burnt muffins.

I felt my jeans pocket and remembered that I'd packed some mirc, not a lot, but enough for some food and accommodation while I was in the PreZone. I stopped in front of what appeared to be a supermarket.

As far as I could tell, it was actually titled 'SUPER Market' but wasn't everything 'super' in the PreZone? What made this place so good?

I dug my now manicured hand into my jean pocket and pulled out my silver purse. I began double checking my savings. One. Five, ten, fifteen, twenty-five, twenty-seven, thirty-seven. That was it, I had exactly thirty-seven mirc and it had to last me at least three days, unless I could find Chance earlier.

Turning towards the opening of the SUPER Market, the automatic doors slid open without a sound, and a voice spoke, 'Good morning Sammy, we hope you enjoy your shopping experience here at SUPER Market.' I screwed my face up, confused and a little scared. How did they know it was me? Just as I was about to turn around and run right out of there, a short man with a bald head and pointed moustache grabbed my arm.

'Don't be afraid. Your first time here, right?' His voice was low and he spoke in almost a whisper. 'Easy, just pretend we're talking about the new Chocolate T,' and the little bald man held up what seemed to be a chocolate, although I'd certainly never seen it before in a tin, and only ever had chocolate on special occasions.

A tall woman with an extremely high bun looked me up and down as she sauntered past. She was holding a green basket filled with tiny tins, each in different colours. While she gave me a disapproving look, she was not overly concerned or bothered with me enough to notice that I was an imposter.

'I don't know what you're talking about.' I tried to brush him off and back out of the SUPER Market, but he stood directly in front of my escape route. How did he know I was from another zone? First time here? I thought I could easily pass for a PreZoner. What, where would I go?

'Your first time here, in the SUPER Market. Don't worry we've only been open a couple of weeks and our customers are regularly confused by Roberta, our robot welcome voice.' I must have exhaled quite loudly and physically relaxed. He was talking about my first time in the store, not in PreZone.

'Oh, yes, she scared me that's all.' The little man winked and let go of my arm.

'Your I.D. Brace, that's how she knows, she scans it on your entry into the store, and then she can welcome you. We're very big on building customer relationships here.' His tiny voice trailed off as I focused on where I was, and where I was, was enormous.

There were rows and rows of tins, each with a different colour label, but no other food, only tins. Where were the vegetables? Where was the milk? The bread? All I could see were hundreds of tins. Did the Prestige eat only from tins? How did they stay healthy? How did they cook? What did they cook? I watched the other customers filling their green baskets with the tins. A young girl with jet black hair and a sharp fringe had four yellow tins. An older man with blonde curls and dark rimmed glasses had two red tins. I must have looked confused again because the moustache man snuck up closer to me and in his low voice reassured me. 'Don't worry I won't tell anyone that it's your first time here! Your friends will never know, you can tell them you're here all the time, I'll even make you an expert. Come with me.' And with that he linked his arm in mine and began to lead me down the first aisle, titled 'A tins', whatever that meant. But the aisle appeared to go on forever and each and every tin was auburn.

'So, on our left we have our entire A tins. A of course for apples, anchovies... oh look we even have apricots to your right.' The moustache man began pointing out random tins and I realised the tins were filled with different foods, all starting with A and colour coded to match. Turning the corner, he continued to ramble, 'Now here we have bananas, beetroot, barley sugar.' We were now in aisle B, where all of the blue B tins were located.

While I was beginning to understand the tin system in the SUPER Market, I was still baffled by why everything was in a tiny tin and there was no fresh food to be seen. We certainly had nothing that even slightly resembled this in AirZone. How did they live like this?

'Continue your shopping. I do not hold it against you for this being your first time here in SUPER Market. I will not tell anyone and be sure to tell your friends about my fabulous customer service.' I flashed him my best smile, which was now perfect, and my breathing slowly began to return to normal. I decided that I needed to get out of there quickly, the whole place was giving me an uneasy feeling.

There was no personality, almost no life. Sure, the small man was friendly, but not genuinely friendly like Mr Franks who mans his veggie stand at the weekend market. Mr Franks, who always gave me an apple for free and asked how my mum was. This place, it may have been 'perfect' to some, but to me, perfectly freaky.

In order not to cause any suspicion I grabbed a couple of purple tins, I didn't even realise what they were until I had left the checkout and had paid ten mirc for them. I only had twenty-seven mirc left, hopefully enough to find somewhere to stay the night, one night at least.

Looking down at the three purple tins, I realised I'd purchased all P foods and now had peanuts, pears and prunes. I almost threw the prunes away. What was I thinking? Yuck! Oh well, I really had no choice and I was hungry, so I decided to eat the peanuts first and save the prunes until I absolutely needed to eat them. As I exited the SUPER Market, the robot voice made me jump again: 'Goodbye, Lawlie.' I froze for about half a second and looked around nervously I didn't want to draw any attention to myself, the robot voice had said 'Lawlie', not Sammy. Had it scanned the wrong I.D. Brace? Did anyone notice?

I was still fumbling around when a tall skeletal woman shoved past me, 'Excuse me, you're in my way.' I mumbled some sort of an apology and scooted right out of there. I tried not to cause too much suspicion, but I knew my face was bright red. I hoped I had not been caught as a PreZone imposter.

Still shaken, I found myself muttering, 'I'm okay, everything's okay,' over and over under my breath until I was far away from the SUPER Market. A park on the corner was mostly empty, except for a couple of PreZone children playing on the swing set. Their parents stood close by, smiling in the sunshine.

I sat down on a bench and pulled the tin lid back on the peanuts. I ate them one by one, trying to make them last as I admired the flowers in the park. Leaning over I smelled the small pink petals and almost ate them, they smelt so good. Instead I picked it to save as a keepsake. But as I pulled it out from the ground, one grew back immediately in its place. I stared in confusion at both the old and the new flower. The new had just replaced the old. I picked a couple more, a blue, a yellow and a green flower and each time they immediately grew back. I wondered if this place could get any stranger. At least the peanuts tasted good.

A loud buzzing noise interrupted my thoughts. My eyes were drawn to an enormous Double U screen in the middle of the park as it flashed on and off. The PreZone children who were playing, and their chattering parents, all stood suddenly straight and turned to the screen intensely.

A rounded face with huge brown eyes stared back at us all from the screen. His bushy moustache and beard were trimmed neat and clean. He spoke in a clear, precise voice: 'Hello, my fellow Prestige, I hope you are enjoying your most perfect day today. It is my great pleasure to remind you all about the masquerade ball that will take place tomorrow night. For those who cannot attend, it will be screened live via Double U screen for all zones to see.' As I watched the man speak, I realised it was Sceptre. But he wasn't in his usual Prestige attire; he appeared more relaxed, casual almost. He must wear the Prestige robes when speaking officially to the other zones – yet another attempt to show his power and elite status. He continued to speak. 'So please, my beautiful Prestige, celebrate with my son and I just how fabulous we all are and just how truly happy we are to not be stuck in any other zone, like so many of them. Thank you and I look forward to seeing you all there.' Then with a grin, somewhat forced, his big bushy beard was gone.

The children and parents continued on with their previous activities and conversations and I exhaled, glad that it wasn't an alert to be on the lookout for a PreZone imposter. I knew I should keep moving. I needed to find a place to stay before it got dark, even though the air would not be locked here. I didn't know who or what would come out after dark and I wasn't about to take any chances.

I walked back along the main street where I found a street by street map of the entire PreZone. It was smaller than I thought, and I worked out that two streets over would take me to some cheaper accommodation. I glanced at my watch – 12.30pm. The day was going by so fast and I needed to work out just how I was going to infiltrate the masquerade ball tomorrow night, and hopefully not wearing jeans (although clean and in one piece). I needed some clothes and a plan.

'Need an I.D. Brace, miss? Got heaps here, all the zones. You look like you could use one. Need one do ya?' I turned around toward the voice and straight into the biggest brownest eyes I had ever seen. He appeared a bit older than me, but not by much, maybe seventeen, eighteen years old? He had short brown hair shaped into a mohawk. He was neat, but kind of rough in appearance, at least in comparison to the clones I'd seen previously walking down the street. He was wearing tight khaki green pants and strong steel capped boots, with a black shirt and grey jacket. In his hand he was holding some I.D. Braces and motioning for me to come and look closer. I moved

'Let me go! How dare you try to kidnap me.' He grinned and stared straight into my eyes, for the second time that day.

'Listen, they're looking for you. That's an imposter siren, and you and I both know you're no Prestige. While we're on the subject, neither am I. So you can either hang around here and wait to be caught and evaporated, or you can hide with me now and try to live another day. Your choice.'

I could hear the siren it was getting louder and louder, closer and closer and what did I know about this PreZone? What did I know about sirens and the law and whether or not they knew I was an imposter? What was it that he said? He's an imposter too? Was he lying? Was it a trick to steal my I.D. Brace? What choice did I have? I had to trust him, so together we ran.

CHAPTER 18

'**WHERE ARE WE GOING?**' I shouted as the strange boy dragged me by my arm along the perfectly built city back roads. We dodged bins and old neatly stacked boxes as we continued to speed down back alleyways and twisted streets, each resembling the last. As we hid behind an expensive red car, we crouched down, huddled together, breathing fast. I was so close to him I could hear his heartbeat, and I was sure he could hear mine.

'Where are we going?' I asked again.

He shooshed me impatiently, and I saw a large motorbike cruise slowly around the corner. I knew immediately who it belonged to. Creepy and silent, like a big red and black spider, ridden by a man wearing a menacing helmet in the shape of a human skull and matching black protective clothes. Skull. The boy and I stared, crouching lower behind the front of the car. The boy began sliding under it and motioning for me to do the same. Creeping past, Skull appeared to be scanning the area. Looking for me, I was sure of it.

We lay flat on our stomachs under the car, the boy's arm pressed around my waist in the cramped space.

I could feel his breath in my face and it smelt like the sweet fruit Cobin and I used to eat. I smiled at the memory for all of a second, until the bike stopped right in front of our faces. I could see Skull's boot with its sharp silver spur, also in the shape of a skull, I clasped my silver necklace in my hand and froze.

He was on his radio. 'All clear down here. I bet it was those sneaky Free Dayers, I really wanted to catch some today. I love it when we evaporate them!' He was snickering, a sinister laugh, reminding me of our last encounter in WaterZone. I shook slightly with fear and the boy's arm gripped around my waist tighter. Stranger or not, the pressure was reassuring. I honestly didn't want him to let me go.

Another voice responded through the receiver, 'Make sure you find them, and evaporate them all. We can't have them running around our perfect zone now, can we?'

'No, sir.'

'And if you don't, Skull, I will have to evaporate you instead.'

Skull paused for a moment before responding. 'Yes, sir. Yes, Sceptre, I will not fail,' and with that, he kicked over his bike and the horrible black and red spider rode off down the alley and turned right. We breathed again.

Rolling out from under the car, I managed to speak, 'Who was Skull looking for? Who are the Free Dayers?'

The boy seemed far more serious now. 'You're not from around here, are you?' He began walking fast and I followed but carefully so as not to be seen.

'Look I know who Skull is. We've got some history. He poisoned my mum and evaporated my friend back in WaterZone. I hate him more than anyone.'

The boy stopped and checked the corner before we continued on, unsure if he was even listening I continued, 'Yeah, so, I get Skull and his agenda but the Free Dayers I've never even heard of. What do they do?'

He continued walking. 'For now, let's just say they're my family, my friends. Skull and his lackeys have it in for us. They catch us and evaporate us and they'll do the same to you, too. I dunno if you realise, but PreZone is a dangerous zone. People die here too, you just don't hear about it.'

Stopping suddenly behind a bin I replied, 'Great, so nowhere is safe.' I tried not to think about Mum and Sammy and we continued in silence. It occurred to me that I might not be making the smartest choice, following this stranger to some unknown location – enemy of Skull's or not. We came to a tunnel. It was an old underground train line opening and I could barely see two inches into the pitch black.

I stopped still. 'We're not going in there!'

He grabbed my arm. 'Yep, don't worry, I know my way. If you're really lucky, we'll get lost and a rat will eat your face off. But don't worry, they're Prestige rats, so they'll use a knife and fork.' Amused, he again pulled me by the wrist into the darkness.

Walking into the shadowy, underground abandoned train track he continued to coax me along. 'Hurry up! It's cool, I know where I'm going. You want to know who the Free Dayers are, don't you?' I wanted to stop and dig my feet firmly into the ground, but I was worried I wouldn't be able to find my way out again or even know where else to go anyway. Plus, the imposter sirens were still sounding in the distance, and it was not my day to be evaporated.

As we descended further and further down the old train lines, it grew darker and a chill began to creep up my spine. The boy moved his grip from my wrist to my hand and sensing my nerves, squeezed it tightly. 'It's okay, these people down here are my friends, and I'm not going to evaporate you.'

I pulled my hand away. 'Ha, that's not all I'm worried about.'

He grinned and looked me up and down. 'Don't flatter yourself, you're not my type. I don't go for annoying, fake PreZoners.'

My walk became more of a stamp as I shot back, 'Yeah, well I don't go for lying criminals who think a little charm will get them anywhere.'

He raised his left eyebrow. 'So you think I've got charm do you?'

I rolled my eyes. 'No, not even close.'

He stopped. 'Yes you do!' He was smirking straight at me.

'Just hurry up, would you. I've got things to do and hanging around in some dank tunnel with you, is not on my list.' I huffed at him. He nodded, still smirking as we continued on down further into the darkness, and me with my hands firmly shoved in my jean pockets.

Turning down what seemed like endless corners and alcoves, some covered in graffiti, some smelling like Cobin's sweaty socks, I began to think about Ryn and his sweet kiss as I boarded the bus earlier this morning. It seemed forever ago, and yet the rush of heat was still fresh in my mind. Was it because he thought I wouldn't make it back? I played this morning's kiss over and over in my head until the boy's voice interrupted my thoughts. We had come to a stop at a huge steel door with the inscription 'Freedom Is Near' engraved across it.

'Now, the people down here aren't really keen on new people, especially ones that could kind of pass for a Prestige.'

'I thought you said I was an obvious fake,' I shot back.

'Look, for your own good, just do what I say when I say it. If anyone gets suss it's not unreasonable for one of them to turn you in for a reward, so keep your mouth shut.'

I had a hundred questions to ask. Who were these people and what were they doing? But I swallowed my curiosity, not to mention my pride, and bit my tongue. A small square peephole opened and a human eye came into view when the boy knocked at the door. 'Password,' the gruff voice muttered.

'Rodney, it's Tyron, let me in.' I looked over at the boy, suddenly surprised that I hadn't thought to ask his name. The owner of the eye grunted and the steel door slowly slid open, creaking and grazing across the dirty ground.

'Tyron, why didn't you say so! How have you been? What's been going on above? Oh, and who's this?' I looked up at a huge, heavy-set man in worn brown clothes with a beard that was far too long and a wide smile.

'I'm–' I began to answer as Tyron put his arm around me and interrupted.

'She's a PreZoner, but trying to cross over. Sick of the life, so she's decided to join the freedom fight with us.'

The large man looked me up and down and still smiling responded, 'Ha, wouldn't want to be around when Firefly sees you bring her in. Good luck my man!'

Firefly? Who was this person now?

Tyron laughed, and patted the bearded man on his shoulder. 'All good, Rodney, don't worry.'

He herded me off into what could only be described as an underground village.

It was busy, really busy, full of people of all different ages and appearance. Some working, making weapons – swords and arrows, some holding guns. I shivered, remembering the Captors from this morning on the bus with their evaporation guns. Some women were cooking, stirring big pots of food, cooking meat on roast racks and music played loudly. 'Tyron, got anything for me from above?' I turned to see an old woman, bent over, with long grey hair and a twitching eye.

'Not today Magna,' he replied, grasping her hand warmly before continuing on past her with his arm around my shoulder, shielding me.

Smiling children in dark, ragged clothes ran in and out of a shop with the words 'Lucky Dip' written on the banner. I could only imagine what was in there, but the children seemed happy enough. I could smell fish and noticed a bucket full of fish heads on the ground as a small tabby cat tapped at them with her paw. A washer woman rinsed out torn clothes in an oversized bucket while two young kids hung the clothes on a make-shift line between two little shacks.

Continuing through the village, dirt caked my shoes and I saw men drinking from mugs and laughing and smiling together as an old accordion player danced beside them. I wondered if the story Tyron had invented about me would hold up, who on earth would leave the PreZone for this filth?

Some people stared as I walked past, and I realised that I was still wearing Sammy's I.D. Brace. I still looked like a Prestige. From the looks on the villagers' faces, the contrast was just as startling to them as it had been to me the first time I'd seen myself in 'Lovely Locks' window. I wondered if coming here was really my best move. A few women began to make comments to each other as we passed.

'What have we here?'

'Oh, I wonder what Firefly will say?'

Tyron didn't seem worried at all and instead walked past them confidently, without acknowledging them.

A few small dogs hurried past my legs, barking and chasing each other until I almost tripped. Tyron caught me. 'Easy there, it's a bit of a culture shock, ain't it? Makes some zones actually look livable.' He was trying to be funny, but I was too overwhelmed to respond. I wished I was home, back in AirZone with Cobin, and I'd even settle for Ryn being there too.

'What is this place?' I asked clearly unnerved.

'Welcome to my home!' he replied, waving his arm at a tiny shack on an odd lean-to the right. He drew back a piece of cloth covering the opening archway. I was surprised at how neat and clean it was. There was a small single bed in the corner with a few matted blankets and a pillow, a chair and table and a few shelves with several books and bits and pieces on them. In the back there was a stove and a fridge in the kitchen area and a couple of bits of fruit on the counter.

'How do you not get your things stolen?' I asked, referring to the hordes of people I saw as we entered the village.

'They know me and we have an understanding here. Plus, I don't have many 'things' to be stolen.' I shrugged, not sure whether to believe him or not.

I sat down on the chair and dropped my backpack onto the floor. He threw me an apple. 'Here, eat this. You must be starving.' I was, and I bit into it, gulping the pieces down fast.

'Woooh, slow down,' he grinned and so did I. It was the first time I felt relaxed since I'd been in the PreZone. He took off his jacket and I noticed just how broad he was as I scoffed down the rest of the apple. He sat down across from me on the edge of his bed, watching me with his huge brown eyes. I was beginning to feel safe when he leaned down behind his bed. I hoped for more apples. Instead, he returned with a small evaporation gun and pointed it straight at me. Unsmiling and serious, his face was frozen and cold as he spoke calmly in a slow, clear voice, 'Now, why don't you tell me who you really are and what you are doing here.'

CHAPTER 19

I ALMOST CHOKED ON the last bite of my apple. 'What?'

Tyron repeated himself, 'Who are you and what are you doing here?'

I glared back at him, furious with myself for letting my guard down. 'You don't need that evaporation gun, I can just explain.' He eyed me suspiciously but still held the gun in my face.

'Just don't try anything, explain yourself and then I'll take you to see Firefly.'

I shifted awkwardly in the chair, why had he changed all of a sudden? What did he want with me and who, who was this Firefly?

'I'm from AirZone. A bunch of us, we ran into trouble in WaterZone. Like I told you, Skull killed my mum and my friend. She's the one who gave me her I.D. Brace as she was dying. So now here I am, in some freaky guy's shack with an evaporation gun pointed at me. What's your story?'

He seemed to relax a bit more. 'What's your name? Your real name.'

'Lawlie.'

He nodded and smiled. 'Well, Lawlie, I'll get a big reward for turning you in for evaporation. So sorry, but your time's up.' He pointed the gun at me and squeezed the trigger. I closed my eyes and waited for the end. But instead, water splashed in my face. 'Gotcha!' He was pleased, taunting me with the fake pistol. I breathed a sigh of relief until my anger took over. I stood up and launched at him, shoving him in his chest, and he spiraled straight back, off the bed.

'You think that's funny, huh? You want me to show you what's funny?' I said holding my hands up ready to sock him straight in his smirking mouth, but he hid behind the bed and waved a white pillowcase.

'Okay, okay, I give up, I'm sorry.'

I lowered my hands, but I didn't care what he said, I wasn't going to forgive him that easily. I jumped over the bed and sent him sprawling onto his back. I started swinging my arms into his ribs as he moved from side to side, attempting to hide from my punches. 'Come on, I said I'm sorry.' He was trying to push me off his stomach, but my legs were firmly holding him in place and he couldn't move me. Then we both started laughing, more relieved than anything. We were acting like kids, our hearts beating from the fight, adrenaline pumping through my body as I could again smell that sweet smell of fruit on his breath as our faces were just inches apart. My eyes had changed from angry to relaxed, his eyes stared into mine as his arms tightened just that little bit more on my legs.

'And what exactly is going on here?' We froze.

'Ah, Firefly, I was wondering when you would greet us.'

I turned around in the direction of the high-pitched female voice that had just entered Tyron's shack. That voice, I knew that voice. It was that same sharp tone from that night at the Waterboard with Ryn. That voice belonged to the woman telling Skull to pollute the water. Firefly was Tash, and she was right here in front of me. Tyron gently pushed me off his chest and we stood up as I straightened my clothes and patted down my hair, embarrassed.

'Tash, hey, this is Lawlie. She's new to the Free Dayers. Lawlie, this is Natasha De'Lane, or Firefly to you.' For the first time I sensed anxiety in his voice. I looked at her long, flowing bright fire-red hair. She was tall and slim with black rimmed glasses and appeared neat and clean, dressed in a black long-sleeved top, black leather pants and the same steel-capped boots as Tyron. She was standing with her hands on her hips, exuding authority. Tash was Firefly. Firefly was Tash. But she was ordering Skull to pollute the water and she was the boss down here too?

She looked me up and down and spoke again: 'So, does she speak or just stand there?' That was it, no one spoke to me like that. I didn't care who she was.

'Now, you—' I started. Tyron grabbed me from behind and covered my mouth.

'Tash, she's just a Prestige trying to be free. Give her a chance, she wants to be one of us.'

Tash eyeballed me carefully. 'No, she *wants* one of us, I think would be more appropriate,' she said slyly, looking at Tyron. I could have punched her right there, but remembered what Tyron had said earlier about keeping my mouth shut.

'Look, I'm new here, I believe in you guys and I want to join. I don't want to cause any trouble.'

She walked slowly over to me and, being taller, looked down at me menacingly,. 'You have no idea what trouble is, little girl.' And with that, she blew a strand of my hair from my face, turned, and as she was leaving the shack, not bothering to turn around she spoke, 'Tyron, she can stay, but she's your responsibility.'

I spun around to Tyron and immediately began interrogating him, 'How do you know her? Who is she? Where did she come from? Is she your boss?' Tyron sat back down on his bed and sighed.

'Well, yes and no.'

I rolled my eyes, that didn't give me anything. 'Yes and no, what exactly? This woman, Firefly, Tash, whatever, is she your leader or does she work for Skull?' Tyron's face screwed up in disdain.

'Skull, never! Why would she have anything to do with him? We all hate him and Sceptre. No Lawlie, down here we run by our own rules.' I scoffed, folding my arms.

'Well, you run by Firefly's rules anyway.'

Tyron, knowing just what I was inferring stood up and stormed over to me. 'Okay, she might be our token figurehead but we are all free down here, unlike up there in AirZone or WaterZone or whatever zone you are from. We don't just succumb to their rules and regulations.' I laughed, mocking Tyron for his skewed views on his beloved Free Day movement.

'No, you only succumb to those that Tash, Firefly, whatever her name is, tells you to. What exactly does she do here anyway?' He shrugged.

'What she does doesn't matter, but it's what she can do that you need to be worried about. You don't ever want to get on her wrong side, and you almost did.' He backed off and sat back down on his bed. I sat down next to him.

'Does she work for Sceptre?'

Tyron laughed, shaking his head. 'I wouldn't let her hear you ask that if I was you. She hates the Prestige, and hates Sceptre the most.' He'd given me a bit to think about, but something was missing, some part of this weird PreZone puzzle.

Tyron paused, as if wondering whether or not to allow me insight into his private world.

'The first time I met Natasha De'Lane was when I knocked on the underground door. She had answered, something she would never do today.' Tyron spoke as if he remembered the day exactly. He continued, 'I remember she actually giggled when I introduced myself. So different to how she is now. She wanted to know what I would bring to the Free Dayers – you know, why they should let me in. She was flirting with me.'

I rolled my eyes. Tyron ignored me. 'I've lived here ever since.'

It didn't really tell me much, but it was a start. I looked up at him. 'Well, what do you people even do here? What does she do exactly?'

He stood back up, rolled his eyes and replied, 'It's probably better if I show you.' And with that he hoisted me up by my hand, and this time I didn't let it go.

CHAPTER 20

UPON ENTERING THE BUSY underground street again, I was immediately drawn back into their world. More children were running around happily, and men were banging steel on steel, molding weapons in a systematic fashion. People continued to stare at me. I was a stranger in their underground world and I was clearly with one of their own, but we brushed past them, just as before.

Tyron gave my hand a tight squeeze and I just acted as if I didn't notice and continued on with him through the busy paths. Skinned bits of animals hung on wires, as a small little hunched back man yelled, 'Mystery Meat here. Get your Mystery Meat here!' On second glance I noticed the meat came in all shapes; long, thin, fat, furry, wait – furry?

Tyron, sensing my trepidation lent over and whispered, 'Don't worry, I'll get you something special from Clouse, he's around the corner he specialises in Special Surprises, slightly less disturbing than the Mystery Meat Bob sells here.'

I shook my head, 'Thanks, but I'm full from the apple.' Whatever this place was, survival was clearly their top priority. Their clothes, their food, their housing were all makeshift. The things that we'd normally discard in AirZone, which was limited at that, would be treasured here. But they all had one thing in common. They were free.

'Tyron, my main man! You want some snakes today?' I froze, staring at a tall skinny man, holding two pythons in his hands, and one wrapped around his neck.

'No thanks Jimmy, I'm fine for today.'

'It's your loss, Tyron,' Jimmy replied with a toothy smile and a wink.

'That was Jimmy,' Tyron attempted to ease my nerves.

'You don't say. Jimmy the 'snake man' no doubt.'

Tyron shook his head. 'No, just Jimmy. Sometimes he's Jimmy the rat man or the ferret man, today he's Jimmy the snake man. Nothing ever stays the same here, the Free Dayers do what they can to survive and use what they can, when they can.'

'And what do you do? Are you Tyron the snake man?' He grinned and squeezed my hand again.

'You saw what I do. I try to fool beautiful, unsuspecting girls from AirZone into buying fake I.D. Braces.'

I glanced at him, as we continued our stroll. 'Are you saying I'm beautiful?' It was my turn to smirk at him now, but before he could answer, a boy stopped him.

'Tyron, can I have one mirc? I needa buy Mum some food for the family and we ain't got enough today.' Tyron reached into his pocket and pulled out two mirc.

'Take this and get enough for you, too.' The small boy's face beamed widely,

'Thanks Tyron!' and he raced off as quickly as he appeared.

'So, this is what you do? Help the Free Dayers, fool the AirZoners and rip off the Prestige?' I pressed.

He shrugged. 'I suppose. I just fell into this life. Stuff happens and you adapt to new situations.' He was clearly brushing the question off, though who was I to talk? I certainly had my secrets too. Yet for all I didn't know about him, he felt real and solid to me. I could feel myself trusting him against my better judgement.

At the far end of the village, we came across an enormous fire with a large podium situated in front. A crowd had gathered, some milling about around the platform, some sitting in the few scattered, rickety chairs that had been set out. Tyron and I took a seat at the back as an older man with a grey beard positioned himself at the podium to address the crowd.

'Thank you all for coming, my fellow Free Dayers. Meeting number 442 is about to begin. Firstly, notes on our previous mission, aptly titled 'Operation No Go.' Richard, can you please update us on the status of this?' The older man stood aside while a somewhat younger man addressed the crowd. He read from his notes.

'Operation No Go was a complete success. We managed to close down several busy streets in the PreZone area including Ray, McDonald and Martin Street. Our blockades worked well to divert PreZoners away from these streets and into Talby, Glenway and Coulter Street where our propaganda team were able to inundate the Prestige community with our message and vision.' The crowd cheered, as Richard nodded and stood down, folding up his notes and taking his seat on the side.

The old guy took over the microphone again. 'Now onto our next area of business. 'Operation C. Radcliff' and that is Chance Radcliff, son of Sceptre, for any of you who had forgotten.' A low murmur and snicker came from the crowd. I almost fell off my chair at the mention of his name as I remembered what my actual plan was.

The old man continued, 'We know that tomorrow night they hold their annual masquerade ball. This year we will infiltrate the ball, kidnap Chance and hold him ransom until our demands are met. However, as this is a far riskier mission with the likelihood of those who fail being evaporated or sacrificed we have had many refuse to partake in this operation.'

The crowd began speaking amongst themselves, their voices gathering momentum as arguments and insults flew at those who refused to partake. But then there she was, the Firefly, with her red hair swarming around her face. Tash took the stage, as the crowd bowed their heads, she took the podium and motioned for them to be quiet.

She began, 'My Free Dayers, certainly one day we will be free and it will be on our terms. I am your leader and I promise you that it will be true. Until that day we live here, in our own freedom and by our laws and by our beliefs. No one tells us what to do and what air to breath. And tomorrow night we break into their masquerade ball and steal the one thing most precious to Sceptre: his son.' Yelling and applause again erupted from the crowd. I didn't think what she was saying was all that different from the old, bearded man who had spoken, but they clearly held her in higher respect than him. That was, everyone except Tyron, who seemed to be bored, as though he'd heard it all before. Glancing at him, he sat silently and watched as the pack continued to shout.

Tash continued, 'Now my fellow Free Dayers, I ask who will join me tomorrow night? I need volunteers. I need brave, strong volunteers who are not afraid to die for our cause.'

I rolled my eyes, if it was so important, why didn't she volunteer?

'Who will risk their own life to kidnap Chance Radcliff?'

The crowd was silent except for one low male voice, speaking up from the crowd.

'I will. I will kidnap Chance Radcliff.' It was Tyron.

CHAPTER 21

'WHAT?' I FLUNG MY head sideways. 'What are you doing?' I was stunned, what did he mean he would kidnap Chance Radcliff – the second most secure person in PreZone? He would certainly die, or at least lose several limbs before that happened.

'I said, I will kidnap Chance Radcliff.' He began moving towards the podium, the horde all turning their dirt-stained faces to see who this mystery volunteer was. Muttering could be heard between the Free Dayers, which soon turned into chanting.

'Take Chance!' 'Take Chance!' 'Take Chance!'

Over and over they screamed, as Tyron climbed the stage and stood next to Tash. She sneered, like she knew more than she would ever let on.

'Well, my fellow Free Dayers, we have a worthy person who will carry out justice for all of us. Tyron Silver. You all know him as your friend and here he stands today, a legend in the making!' She flew her bony arm up into the air and the mob loved every minute of it. Yelling and lighting torches to wave in the air, they followed her like some sort of cult leader. Tyron didn't say another word, I suppose he didn't need to, their leader had spoken and he had just volunteered to kidnap one of the least kidnappable people in PreZone. I knew how this would end and I didn't want to see any more.

I stood up from my chair and attempted to leave, I could infiltrate the Prestige myself without their ridiculous kidnapping plans. Tyron could see me starting to leave and jumped down from the stage and started to run after me. 'Lawlie, wait, where are you going?' I didn't turn around, I didn't want to look at him, how do you look a dead man in the eye?

'Leave me alone, I'm leaving.' I started to stalk along the ground, power walking with my arms firmly pinned at my sides. There would be no hand holding now.

'What's wrong? I thought you'd be pleased. Don't tell me you like the Prestige?'

I spun around. 'No, I don't like them, but I don't think wasting your time kidnapping Chance Radcliff is a good idea either. It's not him anyway, it's his slimy father and his cronies that enforce the rules, not Chance.' He smirked again and this time it wasn't so cute.

'Oh, I see, you don't want Chance hurt. Why not? Do you think you could convince him to change the rules and air would be free flowing in all of AirZone so your family and friends wouldn't die?'

At that second I had enough, and shoved him as hard as I could in the chest, sending him backwards but not over. He got off lightly, I could have punched him. 'Don't you ever mention my family or what I would and wouldn't do for them. Let me go.' And with that, I pushed past him and continued to storm out of there. That was, if I could find where I came in. But he didn't follow me or chase me. I didn't know how long he stood there, as I didn't turn around to check, but I hoped it was a while.

It took me about five minutes and I was officially lost. Every corner, every turn, looked the same as the last and I decided I wouldn't risk asking anyone for help. I knew I had to blend in better. My clothes were alright, by now they were covered in dust and dirt, but my hair and face made me stand out. Not to mention my full set of teeth, unlike a lot of others in the village. I didn't want to get mugged for my I.D. Brace and I certainly did not want to be killed down here and turned into food on a stick, so I knew I had to act fast. Trying to find a quiet place was hard enough. I dropped to my knees and scooped up a handful of dirt. I rubbed a bit over my face and in my hair. I didn't want to know how bad I looked, but finding a glass window I stared at what used to be a normal looking person. All I saw now was a scared girl from AirZone with a PreZone I.D. Brace and no friends to help her.

I walked some more, knowing I had to find food and a place to sleep tonight. I cursed myself for leaving my bag in Tyron's hut, remembering my two tins of food from the SUPER Market and my leftover mirc. It was clear I wasn't going to be able to find my way out of the Free Dayers' village and would have to wait until tomorrow when they left to infiltrate the masquerade ball. At least I had a plan: food, sleep and tomorrow – follow.

With my head down, I continued on my search for food. 'What'll it be, girly?' a deep raspy voice asked as I neared a stall titled 'Grub'. I looked over the jars on the bench: a dead piglet, a dead rat, a dead – I didn't even know what the third one was. I looked down at my clothing, I didn't have anything to trade except, well, except my necklace.

'I need some food and I don't have any money, but I could trade. I've got this necklace, surely that would be worth something?' The man looked at me closely. I unclipped my silver necklace from the back and held it out in front of his bulging eyes. His moustache twitched as he examined it.

'Hmmmm, okay, what do you want? Piggy? Ratty? Doggy?' Yuck, so that was a dog in there. I didn't want any of those, but knew I had to eat something.

'What about fruit or nuts do you have any of those? I could eat those.' He paused for a moment as if running a list through his large head.

'Well little lady you're in luck.' And with that, he rummaged around below the counter and pulled out a small jar of what seemed to be nuts. I reluctantly handed him my necklace and took the jar in my hands and I slipped it into my jacket pocket. 'Good luck, little lady. Sweet dreams,' he called after me in a sarcastic voice that sent shivers down my spine.

It wasn't hard to find a place to sleep for the night. Although the paths and stalls were busy, back corners and behind some of the shacks were free of people, most Free Dayers, I assumed, wanting to get some sleep before the big day tomorrow.

I squeezed in between an old brick wall and what seemed to be an abandoned hut, laid out my jacket on the ground and sat down cross legged with my jar of recently acquired nuts. Twisting off the lid, I sniffed at them. They smelt woody, like saw dust. Shrugging I poured out some into my hands and was about to pop them into my mouth when a familiar voice startled me. 'I wouldn't eat those if I was you.' I turned around as the nuts rolled out of my hands. It was Tyron.

'What do you want?' I tried to sound mad, but I couldn't help but be happy that he had been following me.

'They're night terror nuts.'

I rolled my eyes. 'What is that supposed to mean?'

He came and sat beside me. 'It means, they will give you the most horrible, terrifying nightmares you could ever imagine. If you're really lucky, you won't even wake up. You will stay locked in a nightmare forever.'

I looked down at the remaining nuts in the jar and screwed the lid back on quickly putting them back in my jacket pocket.

'Well, what am I supposed to eat now? And how long have you been following me?' He pulled out a banana and another apple from his backpack.

'Long enough to know you need a bath and that your trading skills need a lot of work. You could have got at least two pigs in a jar for that necklace.' I shrugged at him.

'Well it doesn't matter. I was hungry and I left my backpack in your hut. That necklace wasn't important to me anyhow,' I lied. I used to think that necklace had special powers and now my neck felt naked without it.

'Well then, I guess I traded my watch for no reason,' he said, dangling my necklace in front of me. I snatched it from his grip and hugged him tightly.

'Oh, thank you, thank you so much! It is important to me and you got it back.' He returned the hug and I knew that we were back to normal.

'Let's just say it's an apology, for, you know how I acted earlier.' I clicked my necklace back around my neck with a smile. 'There's no point in trying to get back tonight, we'll probably get mugged. Word has spread that you're here and we don't want to be roaming around these streets now, or we'll have more than Jimmy the snake man after us.' He took off his grey jacket and laid it on the ground, motioning for me to lie down, I accepted.

I didn't want to re-hash old arguments and instead lay next to him on his jacket, my head resting on the inside of his shoulder. His arm was draped around my body and I could feel his fruity breath in my ear as he filled me in on who was who and who was doing what tomorrow night.

Eating my apple and banana happily, I snuggled next to him for warmth as he told me about The Free Dayers' plan for the masquerade ball. The Free Dayers seemed to think that they would do all this apparently without any of them getting killed, I strongly doubted that.

I wondered if I should tell Tyron about Tash and how I had overheard her with Skull in WaterZone. Did he already know? After some to-ing and fro-ing in my mind I realised it was better to keep it to myself. After all I didn't know Tyron at all.

He continued to tell me all about the Free Dayers and their grand plans for the future of the zones but I was fast asleep in his strong arms, and for once I didn't have to set my clock to wake up at 6.01am.

CHAPTER 22

Instead of my alarm clock, a rooster woke me up and I remembered exactly where I was. Turning over I looked up at Tyron's face, his eyes were closed and his mohawk was still intact as he breathed quietly. His arm was still draped over me and I really didn't want to have to move it. Wiggling out of his grip his eyes opened. 'Hey, what are you doing up?' he mumbled still half dazed from sleep.

'I need to use the bathroom.' His cheeky grin appeared.

'Good luck,' he replied. Squeezing out from under his arm, I set off to find a toilet or something, anything that even resembled one.

It didn't take me as long as I had first thought it would, and I made a make-shift toilet behind an old empty hovel. On my way back, I thought about Cobin and Ryn and what they would be doing now. Did they miss me? I wondered if Cobin would believe me when I told him everything that had already happened and was still to happen? Would he like Tyron? Or would they try and kill each other? I didn't have to think about what Ryn would think of him, there would be an immediate fight and I'm not sure who would win.

They were both so similar. I couldn't help but laugh to myself.

I returned to our spot by the bricked wall, Tyron hadn't moved at all. 'So what's the plan for today? Do you guys warm up, and do some sort of pre-attack ritual? Do you even have a back-up plan for tonight if Plan A fails, or is it just a whole lot of you storming the ball?'

He continued to lay on his back, staring up at me as I stood over him, my hands on my hips. 'Nah, we prepare. That's one thing we're good at, preparation. We have to be, we have to be smarter than them and we are.'

I laid back down next to him, burrowing into the same warm position as before. 'And what if something goes wrong? I mean, people will die, be evaporated.'

He tensed up and turned his head towards me. 'Yeah, that's why we have to get to them first, starting with Chance.' I turned my head to face his eyes, I needed to see if he really believed what he was saying.

'You can't kidnap him, Tyron. You just can't,' I whispered in an almost pleading voice.

He snorted sarcastically. 'Why, because he's got a good heart? He may do bad things, but deep down a heart of gold?' His voice was mocking.

'He's not like them, I know it, he's different.' I wanted to tell him about Chance's sister, Sammy, but it probably wouldn't change a thing.

Narrowing his eyes, Tyron's appearance changed and he spoke slowly, almost in a whisper, outlining each syllable, 'He is not different, I can promise you that.' And with that, he stood up abruptly, threw on his backpack and, without turning around, spat out, 'Are you coming or not?' I stood up and followed him.

What choice did I have? I knew that there was more Tyron wasn't telling me about Chance, but for now I would have to be patient and follow my own plan. At least now I had a way into the masquerade ball.

Arriving back at the podium and now burnt-out fire, we found three boys, not much older than Tyron sitting at an old wooden writing desk. They were each wearing large, old-style headphones and madly scribbling on a pad of paper. Walking over to them, Tyron shook their hands as the brown-haired boy motioned for us to be quiet. Another boy with a short crew cut handed Tyron one of the headphones and upon placing it to his ear he drew me in close, until our faces were almost touching. I could hear two voices through the headphones; an older man, who was clearly angry, and a younger boy with a softer, clearer, calmer tone. I knew immediately who it was, it belonged to Chance.

'You have no idea what you have done by allowing her to escape. Now I have no one to sacrifice for the Burning of the Light! I trusted you and I thought YOU would be responsible. How dare you make a fool out of me!' Sceptre's loud voice poured into the headset and I could picture his furious face.

'You can trust me, Father. It was a mistake and I have apologised. She just escaped.' Chance sounded apologetic and almost a little sad.

Sceptre continued to berate Chance, 'I will have to fix your mistake at the ball tonight. I will simply have to find another to replace our 'lost' sacrifice.'

'Father, I told you the truth, she outwitted me. I would never betray you, she did escape just like I said. We will find another sacrifice.' His voice was calm, and so, so sad.

Tyron gently pulled the earphones away from both of us and handed them back to the crew cut boy.

'Do you believe me now?' He stared at me, waiting for a response.

'You have the Prestige bugged? So what, Chance probably let her go, whoever she was. He was just saying what he thought his father wanted to hear.'

Tyron laughed. 'You're so gullible, Lawlie. He's just as bad as his maniac father. They wanted to sacrifice some poor girl for the Burning of the Light Ceremony at tonight's ball. To prove their power, their greed, they would evaporate an innocent girl in front of all of the zones.'

I stared back, refusing to back down and refusing to believe such lies. 'Chance let her go, I know he did. He saved her.'

Tyron came closer and I could feel his hot breath on my face. 'Yeah well another girl will just take her place. Maybe it'll be you.'

As I was about to retaliate, flaming red hair caught my attention, as Tash yet again interrupted us, 'Oh, it's you again.' She still looked immaculate, now wearing a shiny red leather dress and pointed heels. She watched us with her beautiful eyes framed by her black rimmed glasses and she once again regarded me closely. 'So sorry to interrupt a lover's quarrel, but we need Tyron to help load the trucks for tonight.' She turned to Tyron, 'Your little friend is welcome to help.' Her tone was cold as she tapped her long, bright purple nails on her hips.

'That's fine, Tash, we'll go now.' He was always so nice to her. I gave her a screwed up, annoyed quick smile. I knew her secret.

I followed Tyron's lead and began to leave, but Tash interrupted again, 'Oh, and another thing, Tyron, I heard the Prestige sacrifice escaped a while ago. They are in need of another girl, approximately

158

sixteen years old with long brown hair and green eyes. You wouldn't know anyone fitting her description, would you?' She stared straight at me, smirking slyly.

CHAPTER 23

I FOLLOWED TYRON IN silence down a long tunnel leading away from the underground city central and, I hoped, as far away from Tash as I could get. The tunnel was not unlike the one I first experienced upon entry to the underground. But other than the fact that I was still underground, I had no idea where I was. We came to a halt at two large trucks half filled with boxes and various crates. He bent down and lifted up a square wooden box, labelled 'Guns' and placed it gently in the truck.

Turning around he froze, and I could see he was shaking slightly as he grasped my arm.

'I think I need to take you back to AirZone tonight – after the masquerade ball. I get this feeling Tash hates your guts.'

I rolled my eyes. 'Oh really, what makes you think that?' I asked sarcastically.

He ignored me and continued seriously, 'You won't be safe here if Tash has it in for you. I will take you back to AirZone and you can destroy the Prestige I.D. Brace. You should never have come here. They will find you if you stay much longer, intruders never last here long.'

'You could find me another I.D. Brace,' I insisted. I sounded desperate because I was.

'There are none, Lawlie. The braces I was selling were fakes. But you have a real one, and it's just too dangerous for you to have a PreZone I.D. Brace at all.' I glared at him, unafraid, and followed him to the trucks. Well if they wanted me dead, they'd have to try their best. I wasn't about to give up now. I may have looked like a Prestige, but I was still Lawlie Pearce.

'I'm going to that masquerade ball tonight, Tyron. I'm going there and I'm going to do what I came here to do. I am not a quitter and I am not scared. I will go through with this.' My eyes were bloodshot and bulging, but I didn't care. I was in too far to stop now.

He slammed down a heavy box and spun around to face me. 'And what exactly is that, Lawlie Pearce? Because you haven't exactly been honest with me from the beginning, have you? Why are you here? And what is your fixation with Chance?'

I bit my bottom lip, a sure sign I was busted and busy trying to think of something, anything, but nothing came to mind.

'That is none of your business and I am not fixated on Chance, I just don't think kidnapping him and holding him to ransom to get to Sceptre is a good idea. Actually, it really, really sucks!'

He came closer to my face and just before he was about to say something he stopped, closed his mouth and turned around, continuing to load the boxes on the back of the truck, he ignored me. Who did he think he was? He wasn't the boss of me.

'Did you hear me?' I yelled at him as he continued to place one box on top of the other, without even acknowledging me. I gripped his shoulder and spun him around.

'I said, I am going there tonight with you to find Chance. That's what I came here to do and that's all you need to know, okay!' His face was close to mine as I stared straight into his eyes and I saw that they were red and sad.

'I'm sorry, Lawlie.'

I frowned and pushed him angrily. 'Sorry for what?' I asked, confused, as he wrapped his left arm around my waist and placed his right hand around my I.D. Brace. Everything went black.

* * *

The first thing I noticed was the smell. It smelt like fuel and it was dark. My hands were tied with rope that dug into my wrists when I tried to wriggle my hands free. I had some sort of makeshift sleeping mask as a blindfold over my eyes and I was lying down on a cushy seat, sort of like a couch.

I pulled sharply at the ropes around my wrist, throwing them into the air and twisting my hands in every direction. It didn't take long for them to come undone. Stupid. Tyron couldn't do anything right. I slipped my hands free and ripped off my blindfold. As my eyes adjusted to the light, I realised I was in the front cabin of the truck. I had to get out of there.

Opening the door, I froze and realised I was out the front of Sceptre's mansion, I was at the masquerade ball. But clearly I couldn't go in there looking as I did. I had to disguise myself. Closing the door quietly, I looked around the cabin for anything that could work as a disguise. I slid over the front seats into the back of the truck and began rummaging around, using the light from the evening as a guide.

There were a couple of old jumpers, stained and dirty, possibly belonging to Tyron, and an old pair of overalls. I knew that if I walked in in those clothes I'd be noticed for sure, no one in the PreZone would ever wear such rags. Digging behind the left back seat, I found spray cans, little packets of dry biscuits and a suitcase. Pulling out the case I read the inscription: 'Natasha De'Lane'. Tash, this was her suitcase, but what was it doing in the truck? Was she planning her escape? Was she running out on the Free Dayers with Skull? I shivered at the thought of even being a tiny bit close to Skull again.

Ripping open the bulky case, beautiful garments overflowed onto the seat. Jackpot! Trading my dirty PreZone clothes for Tash's, I emerged from the back of the truck dressed in a shimmering red ballgown. It was strapless with tiny black sequins stitched around the bodice. I had laced up the corset as best I could and the layers upon layers of petticoat helped to hide my sneakers. It was beautiful, too beautiful for Tash, I thought. I tied my hair up into a bun high on my head and looking at myself in the rear vision mirror, I knew I needed a mask. Time was running out fast, so I used the black sleeping mask Tyron had used to blindfold me and cut two holes out for eyes using manicure scissors, also courtesy of Natasha De'Lane. I gently sat it over my face – perfect. I scrubbed the rest of my face clean using some left over bottled water and an old rag. No one would be able to tell who I was, not even Tyron.

I took a long, deep breath, and thought about Cobin, Ryn, Mum and Sammy... all gone. This was it. Silently slipping out of the front cabin of the truck, I could see the entrance to the ball in the distance. There were glowing coloured spotlights and music playing. Cars were lined up, one after the other. I could see PreZone couples arm in arm, dressed immaculately, floating in, giggling and beaming. I snuck closer, hiding behind a large tree. How was I ever going to get inside?

I knew I couldn't simply walk through the front door. I did not have an invitation and I also had no partner, also suspicious. Crouched behind the tree I could hear my breathing increase, faster and faster. Think, Lawlie, think! Then I saw him. It was Skull. He was dressed in a black tuxedo, wearing an earpiece and visible evaporation gun with that menacing skull emblem on his jacket. He was manning the front entrance, talking to two other equally large Captors in suits, looking very serious and intimidating.

Great. I hated that guy, what was I going to do? I would have to cause a distraction. I needed to get those goons and Skull away from the front door so I could slip in, quietly and fast, without detection. Not too far away, more PreZoners were arriving in their shiny cars. A couple got out of a small black car far too close to me, laughing together as they made their way to the mansion. They didn't lock the doors.

I ran over to the car and climbed inside. I had never been in an actual car before, we didn't have access to them in AirZone, and the unfamiliarity of it had me confused. The inside was empty apart from a screen. 'Great, how does this even work?' I pressed the screen and it flashed green immediately, with a large round circle complete with mouth and eyes staring back at me. Its mouth began to move.

'Do you want to drive?' a robotic voice asked me and I smiled, yes, I certainly did, right down that hill!

'Yes!' I said directly to the round face.

'Okay,' it replied as I jumped out of the front seat and it began to roll.

I sprinted back to my hiding spot, knowing that when it was time, I had to run, and run fast. It looked approximately five meters to the entrance and I needed to make it without suspicion. The car was moving quickly.

I watched from behind the tree as it rolled down the hill, just skimming several other overly expensive cars. Switching between the car and Skull, I waited patiently for my exact moment to go. And there it was. BANG! The car smashed straight into the giant oak tree. Skull's eyes shot across to the tree and yelling at his men, they began to head straight for the car, evaporation guns out. Okay Lawlie, run! I could hear my own voice in my head, screaming at my legs to bolt. As fast as I have ever moved in my life, I headed straight for the front door. Everyone in the vicinity of the area was crowding around the smashed car, confused and curious. I just continued to run, straight to the front door without stopping, and breathing fast.

The door was unmanned and I glided straight in. Controlling my breathing, I smoothed my gown and patted my hair and for a moment I stood in awe at the eccentric room I had just snuck into. 'Okay Lawlie, let's do this,' I muttered to myself as I took my first step into the great Prestige ball.

It was unlike anything I had ever seen before. Looking up high above my head, I saw large high ceilings with chandeliers hanging, glistening in the light. Across the walls were paintings of past Prestige, staring down with smirking faces. I was surrounded by beautiful looking people wearing immaculate gowns and suits, giggling and amused, sipping coloured fizz from their diamond encrusted glasses.

For a moment it felt as if everyone had frozen for just a second to stare at me, faces peered from behind extravagant masks, woman whispered into partners ears and looked me up and down in awe. I didn't want to stand out, but apparently I looked a lot better than I had thought in Tash's dress and my handmade mask. It was then that I felt his gaze, before I fully realised who it belonged to. Chance had seen me enter from where he was standing, looking down at me from the top of the stairs. He wasn't wearing a mask and his black hair was neatly brushed back in place. His jet black suit and white shirt almost glowed, it was so perfectly bright. He was staring... at me. I stared back at him and couldn't help but smile, after all I now had the attention of the most gorgeous person in the room and his eyes wouldn't leave me. I could feel my face heating up, glad that I had my make-shift mask on.

I knew I had to speak with him, I had to tell him about Skull and Tash and Sammy and somehow I had to push my way through all of the Prestige on the busy dance floor and get him alone. Just as I was about to head straight for the stairs, a tray of glasses each filled with multi-coloured fizz interrupted me and I lost my view of Chance.

'Drink, Madam?' I spun around and came face to face with Tyron. He was dressed in a waiter's attire, his mohawk was gone and his hair neatly brushed to one side. I was surprised at just how attractive he was, when he cleaned up a little.

'Ah, yes, thank you,' was all I could manage to mutter back. Even though he looked amazing, I was still furious at him for what he had done earlier and knew that I couldn't let him think he'd won.

'You're welcome, miss.'

I smiled slyly back. 'Nice suit.'

He stared at me for half a second, put down his tray of fizzy drinks and lifted up my mask.

'Lawlie, you – you look – you're beautiful!' If I hadn't been so mad at him I would have been pleased to hear him say those words, but I had to focus, and beautiful or not, I could still kick his butt. I brushed his hand away from my face and moved the mask back into place.

'Don't touch me, traitor. As far as I'm concerned, we're done. You and your loser Free Dayers had better leave before I tell everyone what you're here to do.'

He leaned in and looked around concerned someone would overhear. 'Shhhhh, you don't understand anything. You don't know the whole story – you shouldn't be here, I am trying to protect you.' I shoved him in the chest again, I was getting really good at that.

'Do I look like I need protecting? Get out of my way.'

I tried to push past him, but he grabbed my arm. A couple of Prestige began to take notice and he let it go, but not before drawing me in close, he pressed his mouth against my ear and I felt his hot breath and that familiar fruit smell as he whispered, 'Don't risk your life for *them*, Lawlie.'

I turned my head and stared him straight in the eyes, and smirked back. 'Don't risk yours.' And at that second, my eyes returned to Chance whose face had now changed, he was now frowning at what he had just witnessed between myself and Tyron and he did not look happy.

Shoving my way past Tyron and the Prestige on the dance floor I began to walk up the giant staircase, heading straight towards Chance. The staircase wound around in a spiral shape up to the second level. I passed stunning women in beautiful glittering dresses, far more exciting than mine, but I knew I could still easily pass for one of them. Two other woman giggling and sipping fizzy liquid from long skinny glasses ignored me as they discussed their dresses and extravagant hairstyles. A woman with a jet black bob cut and stern fringe narrowed her eyebrows and pointed at another Prestige across the room. Her friend with long bright yellow and pink curls cackled in a theatrical manner at something she said and turned her head in disgust. I could only assume they were making fun of the other woman and just thankful they didn't notice me. But I had been distracted by the gossipers and Chance had disappeared. I needed to find him fast – it wouldn't be long before Skull realised that my distraction was a stunt and began scoping the room for the intruder.

I walked along the balcony on the building's second story, and could see the entire dance floor from a bird's eye view. It was magical, just as I had imagined it would be back when I daydreamed about it in my bedroom in AirZone. Men and women were dancing to the sound of a classical orchestra and waiters zig-zagged in and out, serving drinks of all different sizes and colours and Tyron was down there, somewhere. I found myself peering in different rooms as I searched the floor, hoping to find Chance and not Tyron and the Free Dayers. One room was locked, while the second was slightly ajar, and with a small push it opened and I was able to sneak in. The walls were covered with beautiful painted flowers, and old dreamscape paintings and prints in every direction I looked. There was a large shining mirror encircled with silver roses and below sat a hairbrush, comb and several small jewellery boxes, again with the embossed floral design. Where was I? I ran my hand over the hairbrush and blew the dust off my fingertips that had appeared. Next to the hairbrush sat a small photo frame with a picture of a woman with long blonde hair, curled with flowers expertly woven through it. Her bright blue eyes couldn't be mistaken, they were Chance's too. I was in Chance's mother's room, staring at a picture of her.

At that moment, two voices entered the room. I quickly ducked behind the chaise lounge out of sight in case it was Tash or one of her Free Dayers.

A rough angry voice interrupted my thoughts and I knew immediately who it belonged to. 'You have no idea what I go through with you Chance. No clue at all. And here you are trying to save all the other zones and for what?' It was Sceptre and like the phone call I overheard back in the underground, he was irate and again, it involved Chance. I stayed hidden behind the lounge and I tried to think of some excuse if they discovered me there. They both entered the room and I could hear Sceptre pouring himself a glass of something.

'But, Father, it's just so barbaric that you take the air, I mean stealing from an entire zone to ensure that we have enough, and for what?'

Sceptre slammed his glass on the table. 'I am ensuring our longevity. Why can you not understand that?'

Chance continued to try and reason with him. 'You and I both know that it's not fair to treat the other zones like this.'

I could hear Sceptre breathing heavily, frustrated with his son as he came closer and spoke in a lower, more hurtful voice. 'And you would do well to remember exactly who you are, Chance Radcliff. Or should I say who you are *supposed* to be. You are my son, and you will do as I say. This is the end of our discussion on this matter. I will not allow the zoning to be altered and I will not, WILL NOT stop the Burning of the Light Ceremony.'

Chance lumbered around the room defeated, saying nothing as I closed my eyes tightly, praying he would not walk behind the couch, but of course he did. He stopped momentarily as he saw me hiding and realised that I had heard every word he and his father had just said. His eyes opened slightly wider in surprise, but he just continued talking.

Chance motioned towards Sceptre and attempted to lead him towards the door. 'Okay, okay, Father, I don't want to ruin this night, after all it's supposed to be a celebration. Shouldn't you be announcing something anyway? I don't want to get in the way of your big speech.'

I heard Sceptre's glass clunk on the table once more and he sighed in either boredom or weariness, I couldn't tell. 'As always son, it was a pleasure speaking with you.' And he turned and exited the room, leaving Chance and I the only occupants. Chance came back around the side of the couch where I was hunched over, he squatted down and offered me his hand.

'It's you, the girl from before.' He was even more handsome up close. He wasn't wearing a mask and his blue eyes shimmered as he smiled and lifted me up by my hand.

'I'm so sorry for overhearing that – your fight with your father. I was lost and I didn't want to interrupt.' He brushed a stray piece of black hair out of his eyes,

'Trust me, it happens so regularly that neither one of us cares who overhears anymore.' I moved around and sat down on the couch and straightened my dress, as he sat next to me.

'I don't believe we've met before, miss…?' I straightened my back quickly.

'Lawlie, Lawlie Pearce.'

He paused, looking at me questioningly. 'And where are you from, Miss Pearce?' I shifted nervously on the couch.

'PreZone of course. I'm living with relatives at the moment.' I knew it sounded made up but I hadn't even thought of a back story.

He continued to watch me closely. 'I don't recall you on the guest list, who are you here with?' Great, I was caught out. This was it, evaporation time. Could I tell him the truth? Would he listen? I looked away, as he poured a glass of water and handed it to me, our hands brushing slightly as I clasped the glass.

'Why don't you take off your mask, show me just who stopped me from breathing a few moments ago from the top of the stairs?' I thought that statement was ironic, considering it was him who could stop us breathing at any time in AirZone. He reached over and slid off my mask. My eyes met his and his perfect mouth smiled.

'You're beautiful,' he almost mouthed the words. I fumbled with the glass and it fell out of my hands and smashed on the floor, I swiftly grabbed his hands as he started to get up embarrassed.

Quickly, I remembered what I had come here to do. 'No, I'm Lawlie, Lawlie Pearce and see this.' I threw my wrist in his face, 'This I.D. Brace belonged to a girl from here, her name was Sammy and she said she was your sister, but you don't have a sister, do you? And she died and she gave me her I.D. Brace and told me to find you. And it gets worse. I also need to tell you that Skull has been secretly polluting each zone's water supply to kill residents and stage an uprising and this Tash woman is helping him. I think they're an item, but that's beside the point and, well here I am, and this is not how I planned it at all.' My voice trailed off as Chance's eyes remained wide with concern.

'So, she's dead?' It took me a moment to realise he was talking about Sammy.

I nodded. 'Yes, I didn't know her for long but she helped us stop Skull and Tash at the Waterboard and then he killed her. She gave me her I.D. Brace before she evaporated entirely.' He looked at me, his eyes wet with tears and ran his hand frantically through his perfect black hair.

'I can't believe she's really gone. And you? Who are you again?' I exhaled a little more easily, he was so confused.

'I'm Lawlie Pearce and I'm from AirZone.'

He sat back down and appeared calmer, he smiled, almost proud of me. 'So, you broke in here? You crashed my father's ball, using my dead sister's Prestige I.D. Brace, Sceptre is polluting the water supply and someone, someone is actually dating Skull?'

I burst out laughing, although it really wasn't appropriate. Chance laughed too at the thought of anyone ever wanting to be with Skull. Our laugher soon faded, ending what could have been an awkward moment, but I continued, 'Yes, that is exactly what I've done, oh and warn you about the Free Day Army that want to kidnap you tonight, but we can get into that later.'

He laughed again, nervously this time. 'What? Kidnap me? Sceptre would have them evaporated in seconds.' My eyes narrowed at his arrogance.

'Yeah, well they're pretty organised. They've already infiltrated this place, so you should be careful, or you'll be evaporated like your sister.' He moved slightly away from me and his face changed when I mentioned Sammy. I didn't intend to sound so mean, but who was he to think he was untouchable? He was essentially just like the rest of us.

He looked up at me, tears starting to form in his eyes. 'Everyone leaves me.' I was assuming he was referring to his dead mother and now dead sister and I instantly felt bad all over again for my comment.

'Look, I sometimes say things without thinking, and–' But I didn't need to say anymore, his hands held mine and we stared at each other as he smiled, his perfect smile, and then I saw them enter the room.

CHAPTER 24

'**LET HER GO, CHANCE!**' We both looked up as Tyron and four of the Free Dayers broke through the door. Tyron was still in his waiter disguise, but now he was holding an evaporation gun. I jumped in front of Chance immediately to protect him.

'Tyron, back off. I told you leave him alone.' I was still holding Chance's hand as Tyron stormed over and ripped him away from me.

'Let's go, Radcliff. You're coming with us.' I put my arms up in an attempt to shield Chance from Tyron, but Tyron shoved past me as one of his shaved headed followers held me to the side.

'Who are you?' Chance fronted Tyron.

'My name's not important to you. None of us are important to you. All you care about is your precious Prestige Zone. Well, I've got news for you, you won't be around to enjoy it much longer.' Tyron motioned for him to move to one side as another Free Dayer handcuffed him tightly. I started yelling, hoping Tyron would see sense, but he ignored me.

'You're coming with us, Radcliff. If you yell, I'll evaporate you. If you try to escape, I'll evaporate you. Basically, if you do anything out of line, you're dead.' Tyron prodded him towards the door. The shaved-headed follower continued to hold me tight. I struggled to break free as Tyron came closer, an inch away from my face.

'What the hell do you see in this guy, huh?'

'Someone who isn't you and that's for sure.'

He grinned in response. 'Are you on our side or are you with the Prestige?' He was so close I could feel his breath on my face.

'I'm with whoever isn't *you* right now.'

He sneered back at me as if he wanted me to change my mind, throw my arms around him and follow him forever. Instead I stared at him in disgust. This was not the way I imagined this night going. His hand touched my face as he clasped my chin in his hand, and leaned in to kiss me. Feeling his face drawing closer I turned my head abruptly and his lips only just brushed my cheek.

'One day you'll understand. Take her with us. Let's go.' He motioned for the shaved-headed Free Dayer to take me with him as he led Chance out, handcuffed through the Prestige crowd and down the huge spiral staircase.

Everyone stopped and stared as Tyron marched Chance, a Prestige, and Sceptre's son, through the ball. Gasps and cries erupted from women as they saw the evaporation gun. The music stopped and it became silent. Everyone had frozen to watch. Then as they were halfway down the giant staircase he spoke.

'And just what is going on here?' It was Sceptre and he was looking up from the dance floor on the ground level. He had pushed his way through the shocked audience. His golden crown shone under the chandeliers as his large brown eyes, so unlike those of his son's, narrowed into a piecing glare. He halted when he saw his son in restraints.

'Chance? Who— What—' His eyebrows furrowed, confused as he looked at his son.

Chance began to speak but Tyron cut him off, 'We're taking your precious son and when we're ready we'll tell you our demands, but I can promise you this, things will be different.'

Sceptre watched Tyron with narrowed eyes and spoke calmly and loud enough for everyone to hear. 'I know who you are and what you want. Yes, you will take him and make your demands. We will comply and then we will seek our revenge.'

Tyron sneered and prodded Chance's back with his evaporation gun. 'And I know you, old man, seems we are both familiar with each other.' I didn't know how they knew each other or what they were talking about, but I didn't have time to think about it as Tyron thrust Chance through the guests with his gun. The shaved-headed Free Dayer had me by my wrists and pulled me behind them.

BANG! BANG! BANG!

Three shots fired, it was Skull who came running through the archway, three Captors on either side. His face was fuming from my car stunt earlier. He wanted justice and he wanted Tyron and I dead. But there was nothing he could do, Tyron had Chance. He stopped, eyes narrowed, and spoke, 'This does not end now, my boy. This will end when I say it does, with you and your little pathetic group evaporated.'

If Tyron was intimidated, he didn't look it, and instead muttered, 'Let's go,' and began moving Chance through the group of now hysterical Prestige with Skull closely behind him.

People ducked, crashed and scattered fast. I could feel the desperation in the crowd as they scampered out the exits. Sceptre's Captors were busy calling for back up into their headsets as I continued to be pulled out into the night air.

Tash was waiting for us in the driver's seat of the same truck

I had previously escaped from. She was amused, with her nasty grin and her eyes wide with excitement. 'You got him, you really got him!'

Tyron threw Chance into the truck, still pointing the evaporation gun at his head. The shaved-headed Free Dayer turned around briefly and was about to shove me into the truck when a Captor shot him straight in the head and he was evaporated. I stood there, half a metre from the truck, stunned. I could see Tyron, his eyes locked on mine. 'Get in the truck, Lawlie,' he demanded from inside, but I just stood there, motionless, unable and unwilling to move.

'I said get in the truck!' he shouted again and pointed the evaporation gun directly at me, but I continued to stand still, staring at him.

'Run, Lawlie, run!' Chance began yelling and Tyron smashed him over the head with the gun, and he fell sideways into the back seat.

'You're one of us, Lawlie,' Tyron continued to scream at me. He was still yelling for me to leave with him as his truck sped away and I blacked out for the second time that day.

CHAPTER 25

'**WAKEY, WAKEY, MY DEAR** little girl. Good to see you again so soon.'

I opened my eyes and squinted as I adjusted to the bright piercing light of the room, two tiny black eyes were staring straight into my own. I rolled back, disoriented at the sight of the tattooed face, wrinkled and dishevelled like an apple that had been sitting in the sun for too long.

'I said wakey, wakey, gorgeous. Time to GET UP!' Skull screamed, inches from my face. I could smell his breath; a mix of old tea bags and fish as it flowed through his overcrowded, decayed teeth. 'Who are you? And you better not tell me any lies!'

SMACK! He kicked me in my side and I lay crumpled on the ground in pain. A sharp sting flew from side to side across my ribs as I cried out.

'I'm Lawlie Pearce! I'm Lawlie Pearce!'

He took a step back and eyed me suspiciously. 'And why are you here, Lawlie Pearce? And why are you intent on ruining everything I do?'

I opened my eyes wider and forced myself to look up into his demented face. It was cold, expressionless, terrifying. His beady eyes flashed as he saw me cringe in pain. A scar across his mouth was evil and shaped as if he had been cut by something, or someone. He was tall and skeleton-like, but nonetheless evil and enjoying every second he tortured me.

'I asked you a question.' He kicked me again in the same exact position. I cried again in agony, wrapping my arms around my body for protection and wishing I could break his legs right off.

'Okay, okay, stop, stop! You killed my mother with your poisoned water! And that girl you murdered in WaterZone? She was Prestige. You deserve everything you get from me!'

'So that's where you got the I.D. Brace. So now you're just following me around like a bad smell, are you?' I lay there staring at him, silently imagining what it would feel like to twist his skinny leg until it broke. 'An intruder in PreZone, you know what we do with intruders don't you?'

I had recovered from his kicks and was more than just a little angry. I scooted myself up against the wall in a sitting position with my arms tightly wrapped around my bruised ribs. If I was going to get to the bottom of the water pollution, I needed to gather as much information as possible and, in doing so, have Skull own up to whatever his role in it was.

'I know about you, Skull. I know you and Tash are behind the water pollution, but I also know you two are just little puppets for Sceptre and that he is the one who is ordering the poisoned water.'

'No, he's not! It's Tash's idea. Sceptre knows nothing about it.'

I smiled. So Sceptre is unaware of these two and their plan. Well I am going to be the one to tell him!

I grinned. 'Well he'll know soon enough.'

He laughed his revolting laugh, realising what he had given away. He pretended to kick at me, as I flinched, preparing for another blow. 'Well, I see you have connected some of the dots, my little friend. But there is nothing you can do about it, especially once I shut you down permanently.'

I frowned and of all the reactions I could have had, I laughed. Not a good response.

'Oh, so you think this is all so humorous do you? I wonder how funny you'll find it when we force Sceptre to hand over his crown. Not to mention when we lock all the air in each zone permanently, starting with AirZone.'

I shook my head from side to side trying to figure it all out, and still shocked that anyone would want to pair up with this psycho.

He paused and watched me closely. 'And how do you know Tyron Silver? You know he is a well-known vigilante in the PreZone. He is one of our ten most wanted criminals.'

'He—I met him on the corner. He tried to sell me an I.D. Brace and then we heard sirens, so we ran and that's where I met his leader, Tash. She is crazy, just like you. No wonder you two found each other.'

'Ah yes, Tashhhh.'

The way he uttered Tash's name made me shudder. I wanted to be at home. I wanted to be with Cobin and I didn't even care if there were AIRLOCKs and curfews, I just wanted to be anywhere but here, away from this skeletal menace.

Skull snorted as he poked me with his giant boot. I recoiled in fear of another strong kick to my rib cage. 'Let me go,' I screamed.

But Skull laughed, his evil mouth curling into a hideous grin as he replied, 'Oh no, you will stay, for you are the entertainment.' He smirked, his crooked teeth poking out from behind his mouth. I rolled over confused and tried to sit up again.

'What do you mean?' I asked, concerned.

But he didn't answer, he just continued to snicker as he exited the room. I could hear his vicious teasing from down the hallway and the stomping of the giant boots that had caused me so much pain. I screamed out after him, angry and determined to not let him break me, 'WHAT DO YOU MEAN I'M THE ENTERTAINMENT? YOU UGLY MONSTER!'

* * *

Skull returned and stared with his beady eyes, uh oh, maybe I had gone too far.

'Alright, Little Miss Painful, you can come with me!' He grabbed my arms and lifted me from my crumpled position on the floor.

'But just so you don't accidently reveal anything to Sceptre, I want to remind you of who I am and what I can do to the rest of your family.' I struggled to pull my arms out of his grip, but he was far too strong. I gritted my teeth and forced myself to stare him down, front on, eyes locked on beady eyes.

'I have no family,' I spoke through clenched teeth.

His smirk returned. 'Oh yes you do. Your little friends back in WaterZone, don't think I don't know all about your two boyfriends and how important they are to you, especially now, since I poisoned your mother.'

I ripped my arms out of his grip, fuming and breathing fast and loud, but he encircled my entire body with his arms and stretched my arms around my back, locking them in place.

'Now, don't you try anything in with Sceptre or your two boyfriends will be evaporated!' He laughed at his own joke as I jerked my body ferociously with one last attempt to break free, to no avail.

'Well, you certainly are strong for your size and annoying, too. Let's see just how tough you are now.' I looked around as he pulled a handkerchief from his pocket, which I really hoped wasn't used, and stuffed it into my mouth. I almost choked on the taste of it.

'I can't have you seeing the way to Sceptre's office now, can I?' He was holding what appeared to be a grubby hessian bag, the type we use in AirZone to store potatoes, was he going to put it over my head?

I felt the rough material encase my face, yep, now I was in trouble.

'There! Now you can't talk or see, but you can hear, can't you?! Hear exactly what I'm going to do to you! I can't wait for you to know!'

I pushed my body around a few more times, attempting to break free, or at least annoy him, but it was just using energy I needed to save. Who knew where I was going after this? I squinted, trying to see through the sack but I could only just see through some of the tiny holes. Maybe that would be enough.

He marched me out of my cell and up some steep, sharp stairs and I realised that I was downstairs, way below where the Prestige had all been dancing and laughing only hours ago. This must be where they hold their prisoners, I thought as he unlocked a heavy steel door.

He continued to push me in my back as we ascended to Sceptre's office. I couldn't see much, other than just the inside of the dirty sack which, just as I suspected, smelt like old potatoes.

He knocked on the door.

'Enter.' I recognised the authoritative voice. Yes, it was Sceptre alright. Skull herded me into the room.

'She says she's from AirZone, snuck in here on a Prestige I.D. Brace.' Skull snickered in front of Sceptre, proud of his own findings.

Sceptre paused, confused. Peering through the sack, I could make out his body and for the first time I could see he was looking a little frail in his oversized chair at an awkwardly large desk. He sighed, obviously not all that interested in me, the intruder, anymore, not since Chance had been kidnapped. There was no one else in the room as he sat in almost complete darkness, just the light from the jewelled desk lamp glowing ominously across his face.

'What exactly was she doing at my masquerade ball?' he asked Skull in an accusing voice.

'I guess she was hoping to stop us or something, stop the AIRLOCK, her mum died, blah, blah, the curfews etc. etc., blah, blah, blah. As if she was ever going to succeed.' Skull pushed me to the side and pulled out a chair and sat down across from Sceptre, placing his large, pristine boots on his desk.

'But she did succeed, didn't she Skull? She did get an I.D. Brace, she did join the Free Day Army, she did crash my masquerade ball and she spoke with Chance, and about who knows what, because now he has been kidnapped on your watch.'

Sceptre stood up abruptly and slammed his fists down on the old desk making me jump. 'IT DID HAPPEN – ALL OF THIS!' he shrieked, at the not so smug Skull, who quickly removed his boots from the desk and sat up straight.

'Yes, but – eh, well, we have her, Your Highness, she is our prisoner,' he choked in reply.

'Yes, and they have Chance! The heir to Virozone,' he bellowed into Skull's scared face.

'What is it that you suggest we do?' Skull began to sound like a frightened little child as he slid out of his chair and slowly backed away, creating distance between himself and Sceptre.

'You will do nothing! I will work out a plan. In fact I may already have one.' Sceptre's voice trailed off.

Skull, still fearful, but determined to succeed, nudged the question in sneakily. 'And the girl?' he asked, his slippery grin slyly appearing as he pointed in my direction.

Annoyed at the interruption, Sceptre replied, 'Do you think I care about her? Evaporate her, kill her, whatever you want. She is not my problem.' He flicked his diamond covered hand in the air, motioning for Skull to leave.

'Might I make a suggestion, Your Highness?'

Sceptre removed his glasses and sighed, frustrated with Skull as he continued with his infuriating questions.

'What?' he growled throwing his glasses across the desk.

'Might I suggest a sacrifice? Since our other girl escaped, perhaps we could replace her. This girl would be perfect. I feel after the incident that occurred in front of so many influential Prestige, we need to show the zones that the Prestige are not easily defeated or shaken and that we are, in fact, continuing our beautiful lives.'

Sceptre shrugged wiping his balding head with a handkerchief. 'Whatever needs to be done.'

Skull grinned an evil smirk with his browning chipped baked bean teeth. 'Excellent. I will make the appropriate arrangements.'

Skull grabbed my arms and dragged me from the darkened room. I could sense he was smiling, no doubt looking forward to watching my death, live for all Virozone to see.

CHAPTER 26

'Now, GET IN THERE and see what else I have planned for you!' Skull threw me into another room, and I wondered what else he could possibly have in mind, especially since evaporating me was pretty much the worst he could do.

He pulled the sack off my head, but left the gross hanky stuffed in my mouth. I looked around the room. It was empty except for a narrow bed, some old clothes strewn across the floor and a Double U screen on the wall. Yuck, this cold, empty room I knew had to belong to Skull himself.

'You think you are so clever.' He was beginning to start some form of rant when a Double U screen flashed on the wall. We both froze at the sight of it flashing and who I saw I could not foresee.

It was the Firefly herself, Tash, and her red hair was looking even angrier than usual.

'Skull! Where are you?' Skull shoved past me and walked up to the screen.

'Here, dear Tash, right here.' I could see her looking beyond him to me. Obviously I stood out pretty clearly in the room.

'Oh, you have my little friend with you. Great, I wondered what happened to her.'

If I could actually speak, I would have completely lost it and berated her about turning on her zone, on all zones to work with this menace, but instead I could just stare at her, eyebrows narrowed, and she knew exactly what I was thinking.

'Yes, Tash, what can I do for you?' Skull was so polite and nice to her, it made me sick.

'I have a little something to show you and your new little mate!' She grinned, without showing her teeth and I braced myself for whatever it was she could possibly throw at me now.

Skull and I watched the screen, unsure and hesitant about what she wanted us to see.

Then the screen shifted and Tash was gone. We were left watching another room altogether. An actual cell, with bars and a hard floor, then I could see bodies and hear familiar voices.

'Wake up!' I watched as Tyron threw a bucket of old dirty water over Chance as he lay motionless in the barred cell. Chance rolled lightly from side to side, groaning and rubbing where he had been hit on his head by Tyron's evaporation gun.

Tyron sat down outside the cell in an old chair, balancing, tipping himself back and forth as he spoke, speaking almost as if to himself, 'Now you listen here, Radcliff. You're damn lucky I didn't kill you right in front of your tyrant of a father, because I can tell you now I've imagined it for so long.' Tyron stood up and began pacing back and forth outside the cramped cell as Chance stared straight ahead.

'Why didn't you just kill me?' Chance sounded defeated, saddened and tired.

'Is that an invitation?' Tyron stopped pacing. 'Because I've always wanted you dead, Radcliff. I hate your family, your Prestige, your pathetic AIRLOCKs and sacrifices. Nothing you Prestige do is for the good of anyone. You just want power, power over everyone in all zones.' Tyron was irate, his hatred for the Prestige escaping through his every breath.

Chance jumped up and flew at the bars. 'Then KILL me. Do it, come on, you hate me so much, just kill me.' Chance was daring Tyron to carry out his words. He knew that Tyron couldn't afford to evaporate him just to fulfill his own wishes. The hopes of the Free Dayers rested on Chance living and being used as leverage in the fight between them and Sceptre.

'You know damn right I can't kill you, Radcliff,' Tyron sniggered. 'You're worth more to us alive. But believe me, once we're done, I will end you.'

Chance gripped the rusty bars with his hands. 'You keep saying how much you despise me and I don't even know who you are. Whatever I have done, whatever I have said, or my father or his henchmen or–'

Tyron cut him off, screaming, 'You are pathetic! You are in the perfect position to overthrow your father and you can't even do that. You just follow along with everything he wants.' Tyron smashed the old chair up against the cell bars, forcing Chance to jump back in shock and in pain as his fingers took the brunt of the wooden chair.

'You're crazy. You don't even know me.' Chance shook his head muttering.

Chance continued, but in a lower tone, 'You don't even know do you? You're so intent on believing what you see and hear on the Double U screens that has it ever occurred to you to ask why I don't look anything like Sceptre?'

Chance was speaking slowly and truthfully, but Tyron wasn't

about to just accept his excuses. 'Save me your sob story, Radcliff I'm sure it must be really hard being you.' Chance shook his head, no matter how much he tried to convince Tyron, he would never make him understand exactly how he felt.

'Well, you try having your mother die before you could get to know her and being sent to live with a stranger, a man who you despise more and more every day for torturing the zones just to fuel his selfish desires. Oh, and to have the one person you love, who you grew up with, your sister, taken away and before you ever get to see her again, you find out she has been evaporated. Okay, you live with all of that every day and tell me you want my life.'

Tyron was silent. Even I hadn't expected that Chance would unload his entire sad life story onto him, and what did he say about Sceptre? Was he Chance's father or not?

'So are you telling me, among other things, that Sceptre is not really your father and that you were taken from your sister and made to be his son?' It appeared Tyron wanted to get as much information out of Chance as he could to try and make an informed decision about whether or not to evaporate him now or later.

'What's it to you? You've already got an image of me in your head. I don't need to try and change that. I know who I am and I have accepted that.'

Tyron was tapping his foot on the floor, trying to weigh up everything in his mind.

There was silence between the two, neither one of them wanting to speak, or knowing what to say. Eventually Tyron spoke. 'How could that even be possible? That no one knows about you not really being his son?'

Chance rolled his eyes. 'Why would they? Sceptre needed a male heir to Virozone and there I was.'

Tyron sighed. This was clearly not how he had planned his conversation with Chance Radcliff to go. He had planned to aggravate him and then be forced to evaporate him, which of course he would tell Tash was a complete accident.

They were both silent.

'Hello, my dear boys!' Tash's long red hair fluttered behind her as she flew into the darkened room.

I wondered if Tyron thought she looked different to when he had first met her years before. Did her red hair used to be shorter and less fiery? Her eyes, encased in black rimmed glasses, were they always cold and empty?

'So, what's going on in here?' Tash demanded, facing Tyron directly.

'You tell me.' Chance slumped down on the floor in his original position as the tall red head grabbed Tyron by his collar and pulled him close to her.

'Do you want to tell me what the hell you are doing in here with him? We're supposed to be carrying out our plan, if you haven't forgotten.'

Tash was angry, angrier than usual, her piercing green eyes pinning Tyron in his place.

'I don't see why we just can't evaporate him.' Tash snorted and grabbed Tyron's chin with her bony fingers.

'Because, dear Tyron, he is our prisoner and he is the son of the Prestige Sceptre, who coincidently controls all of Virozone. He says when we breathe, when we drink, when we eat, when we have curfew, when people live and when people die. Need I remind you of just who those people are who have died?'

She squeezed his face tighter and he pulled away sharply. 'No, I understand. I live with it every day. We will do this. Tell me what I need to do.'

Tash turned directly to us, she knew we had watched the entire scene and she smirked her slimy grin as she spoke, 'First of all, tell Sceptre he can evaporate the AirZone imposter.'

* * *

Skull turned towards me, turning off the Double U screen. 'See, even Tash wants you gone.' I couldn't respond verbally but I was sure my eyes said enough. 'I've got to organise a few things for the ceremony tonight, and now you're the main attraction! I'd tell you not to go anywhere, but I'm pretty sure you can't anyway!'

He exited the room as I looked around for something, anything to help me escape and then I grinned. Ah, ha! I walked over to the Double U screen and maneuvering my elbow I clicked it on and it lit up immediately. I found myself in Tash's office, watching her every move.

She sat in her office, well, what could be described as a make-shift office, same as everything else in the underground. Her desk was slightly on a lean and the wood was worn and slowly decaying. There was probably the beginning of a slight smell steaming from it, but obviously she didn't care. She probably liked it, the smell of death.

Sitting across from her was the taller Free Dayer from earlier. With his shaved head he was sickly thin, but I could tell she liked having him around, he probably worshipped her, and I'm sure Tash loved that more than anything.

'So tell me what do you make of this whole situation?'

The Free Dayer scratched his head and coughed. 'I think it's going well Tash, like all your plans. We have Chance, we will trade him and you will rule Virozone.' Tash sat up a little straighter and pointed her chin out, swallowing loudly.

'Hmm, yes I will, and what should be the first thing I should do as their leader?'

'Whatever you wish to do, Tash.' Tash smirked, he had answered correctly as she knew he would.

'Yes, yes, yes of course I will.'

'So, you will stop the AIRLOCKs then?' he continued. What was he doing? Tash froze and her slimy smile changed into tightly pursed lips, a look more suited to her face.

'And why would you think that?' Each word she uttered was short and stern; he had said the wrong thing.

'Oh I mean, if you want to. Or not, you can do whatever you want.' He was getting anxious and I could see his pale white hands sweating.

Tash stood up and walked over to where he was sitting, she crept around him and stopped directly behind him, placing her hands on his shoulders she began to press her fingers into his bony shoulders. 'You need to understand, my dear, that I do not and will not ever take advice from you. Do you hear me?' She squeezed her hands into his skin and dug her nails in deep. He let out a slight squeal in pain, but tried to hold it in as much as he could, in fear of a worse punishment.

'So—sorry Tash I wasn't thinking. Whatever you do will be awesome, no one will ever be as good, as great even, you will be amazing.' He was talking fast. I'm sure he was hoping she would unclaw her nails from his skin.

'I know. Now, go and get me Sceptre on my Double U screen, we need to have a little chat.' He jumped up immediately from his chair and ran out the door, but Tash stopped him.

'Oh and.'

He skidded to a stop and spun around, 'Ye—yes?'

She leaned back against her bulky desk and smirked. 'This was a warning, you hear me? Next time, you and your entire family will be evaporated, okay?' Trembling he nodded quickly and continued to run out of the room.

Tash continued to sneer as she tapped her long nails on the desk.

I heard the door lock turn before I could manage to get my elbow into position to turn off the screen and Skull walked in.

'Oh, so you're interested in spying on us too, are you?' I stepped back away from him.

'Never mind, I want you to see all this anyway.' He approached the screen and flicked a microphone button. 'Hello, dear Tash?' Tash jumped at the sound of Skull's voice and I almost laughed at her being scared for a moment.

'What? I've told you not to do that. What do you want?' She was still as angry as before, possibly even more so.

She looked over at me. 'Oh it's you again, are you beginning to see just how powerful I am!' She laughed, enjoying every moment. I wanted to retaliate but again, the rank handkerchief was lodged in my mouth and of course she could see that, and loved it.

'Skull, while I have you here, tell Sceptre he has a call. I want to speak with him now. You two are welcome to watch the entire show. It might be the only entertainment you get, little one.'

Why was she always calling me little? It was only her hair that

192

made her seem bigger, and I would still kick her butt, when I got out of this place.

Skull agreed and covered my face once again with the stinky bag and hauled me out and back into Sceptre's office. He must be pretty anxious around him, he knocked again, more tentatively this time.

'Yes. What now?' Sceptre's voice was slightly more annoyed this time.

Pulling me into the room, Skull spoke, 'Ah, excuse me, sir, for another interruption, but you have Natasha De'Lane on your screen. She, ah, she demands to speak with you.'

Sceptre stood up abruptly and switched on the screen, he could see Tash's face on the Double U screen as he stood in darkness in his room.

'Sceptre, you there? Where are you?' Her bossy voice blasted through the screen.

'Yes, yes, I am here. Where is Chance?' He was desperate.

'He is here, and he is safe, for now. Here's what is going to happen. You are going to announce to the zones that you are renouncing your title. That you are done, finished, it is over. You will give your title to me and I will be the new leader of Virozone.' Tash was to the point and without emotion.

'And what will happen to me? To Chance? To my PreZone?' His voice was uneven, his eyes sharp.

Tash stared, detached. 'You will disappear, I don't care where, but if I see you, for any reason or should you or your cronies try and overthrow me, I will have you evaporated.'

Sceptre rubbed his hands over his face as he considered her offer, rolling his skin around in his hands as if trying to come to a resolution.

'So what will it be, Sceptre, your power or your son?' Tash, still stony-faced, reached across as the Double U screen followed her. 'And just in case you were having trouble deciding, take a look at what you would be giving up. Tyron, bring him in.' Tyron came into shot, pushing a shackled Chance from behind as Tash grabbed him around his collar and pushed him closer into view.

'Hi Dad, look, I—I'll understand if – well, it's a lot to give up, for me.' Chance's voice was almost pleading as he spoke.

'I choose my son. Now, let him go, you can have it all, just give me back my son.' His voice was low and calm, defeated.

Tash pushed Chance out of sight. 'Very well, make the announcement to the zones and if you or him try anything I will evaporate him immediately and then come looking for you, Sceptre.'

He may have been old, but he wasn't stupid, Sceptre interjected, 'Now you just wait a minute, missy. I will make no announcements until I have my son in front of me. How do I know he is not dead already and all of this is just a pre-recorded hologram?'

Tash smirked. 'Okay Sceptre. We will trade. We will meet at the Citadel where the official Burning of the Light sacrifice takes place, say in exactly one hour? There you will make your announcement to all of Virozone and I will give you back your beloved son.'

Sceptre nodded. 'Alright, that is what we shall do. I will have my men organise the live stream to the zones and my title is yours to do what you will.'

Tash grinned, a little surprised at just how easily he folded. Then he spoke.

'Oh, and one more thing, but you might want to call your sidekick in for this.'

Tash was confused and frowned as she motioned for Tyron to come into view.

Annoyed, she questioned him, 'What is it?'

Sceptre spoke, 'Hello Tyron, I just thought that while your fearless leader was making so many demands you might want to see what I plan to do with your new little friend.' Tyron's eyebrows narrowed.

'Here she is, Tyron.' Sceptre spoke pointing at me and I was certain, even with the bag covering my face that Tyron was not stupid, he knew it was me.

'She's also going to meet us at the Burning of the Light Ceremony as our official sacrifice. Now what do you think about that?'

Tyron watched the screen intensely as Skull dragged me into the shot and I yelled as loud and clear as I could with my mouth blocked, 'Tyron – going to – evaporate me – Tyron!'

Tyron ran at the screen, his eyes blazing as he shouted, 'You let her go, she has nothing to do with this. It's between us and you, old man. LET HER GO!'

Sceptre raised his eyebrows and smirked. 'I'll let her go when you let Chance go. But you see, I doubt your leader has the same connection with her as you and probably won't care if she lives or dies. I'll leave it up to you both to sort out. I have an important meeting at the Citadel and can't be late. Until then.'

Tyron faced Tash as she spoke, 'Now, you can't possibly think I will give up being ruler for some pathetic AirZoner, can you Tyron? I mean, it's our time now, baby, to rule the zones and who cares if she's evaporated? I mean, really who is this girl?'

'Someone who is going to evaporate you one day, of that I can be certain.' And with that Tyron attempted to push past her, just as Tash put her hand in front of him to stop him.

'I thought you might try this, lover boy. So, please don't take it personally, but I have bigger plans than you can ever imagine. Boys! Grab him and throw him in with Chance.'

I watched the screen as Tyron nervously glanced from side to side at the Free Dayer boys as they grabbed him by the arms. He pulled out of their grip and punched the smaller one straight in the mouth. Keeling over, the boy groaned in pain. The other, slightly taller, came at him with a long-rusted piece of piping and smashed him in the knee. Tyron went down screaming in agony. Hoisting himself back up, he hobbled with one bent knee and threw a punch, but missed as the Free Dayer stepped back and jabbed him straight in the stomach. Together both boys pulled him into the cell and he landed on his back on the hard concrete floor.

'Good to see you again,' Chance muttered sarcastically as he lay next to Tyron who was bleeding and crippled on the ground.

Tash slammed the cell door closed and leaned her porcelain face up against the bars as she spoke in almost a whisper, 'It didn't have to end like this, my love, but I knew from the moment I saw you with her that I was no longer yours. I could never compete with her. Tell me, my love, what is it about this one, how is she different somehow?'

Tyron sat up on his elbows and hoisted himself up; hobbling on one leg he pushed his face to hers between the bars. 'You really want to know, Tash?' Tash's face tensed as she grimaced in anticipation. Tyron continued, 'She doesn't let anyone fight for her, she fights for herself. I'll guarantee she'll kick your butt once she's done with Sceptre. You hear that old man! She's coming for you next!'

I couldn't help smiling at that and watched as Tash grinned and leaned in closer and kissed Tyron briefly on the lips. He pulled away, as if he had never noticed how cold they were until now and she snorted, 'Goodbye, my love.' She turned and disappeared out the door, leaving both Chance and Tyron in silence. Skull and Sceptre stared at me and I was raging and that was definitely my preferred status.

CHAPTER 27

SCEPTRE WAS THE FIRST to speak, 'Skull, take our new friend back to wherever you brought her from and let's get organised to move to the Citadel.'

I realised that Sceptre still didn't know Tash and Skull were working together and maybe, just maybe, if I told him, I could stop all of this from happening.

'Sceptre, Skull and Tash,' I mumbled but the dirty hanky got shoved further into my mouth.

'Wha—what is she saying? I can't hear a thing with that sack and muffled voice.' Sceptre was curious, but Skull was sly.

'Nothing, nothing. Who cares what she is muttering? Don't you have to address the zones, sir, inform them of your plans? You have more important things to do than worry about her.' I was still trying to yell through the hanky as Skull threw me back into his room.

I knew it was his room from the smell. Did he ever wash?

He removed the sack and hanky after securing the door behind us, there was no way I could get out.

'Lucky he didn't hear what you were trying to say. I really want to see you become the sacrifice!' He was busy gathering items into a bag, evaporation guns, clothes, he was preparing for my death.

'Now you stay in here while I get everyone organised, and don't bother trying to escape, because, well, because you can't!' He laughed, slamming the huge door behind me as I heard the lock click over.

I scanned the room for any way out, or anything I could use as a weapon, but Skull had taken pretty much everything. But he had forgotten that I can access the Double U screen.

I ran over to it and switched it on. Just as I had hoped, Tash had not signed off from her previous conversation with Skull and I could see precisely what Chance and Tyron were doing, although it didn't look like much with them both slumped on the cell floor.

'What are you looking at?' Tyron sat on the icy concrete floor, a far enough distance away from Chance, well as distant as possible in their cramped cell.

'Well, it looks as though I'll be getting out of here and you are now in here, probably to die a slow death, or you might get lucky and she may evaporate you. Who knows?' Chance was only half joking, probably still trying to understand what Tyron had against him anyway and why he held such a grudge for so long. Chance had hoped he could see his side of the story and understand just how much he had not wanted his position of power.

Tyron shot back, 'I don't care about me or you, only Lawlie, and you should too. She tried to save your pathetic Prestige butt, and what do you do? Don't even bother about her; you just want your precious life back, safe and sound with Daddy.' Tyron spat out each word, refusing to look at Chance, and instead digging his heal into the rough ground as if trying to dig his way through the concrete.

'That's not true, I care, I care about her, but I hardly know her.

I mean, other than that she got Sammy's I.D. Brace and broke into my Prestige party. But you're right, there is something about her: she – she's different.' I smiled, watching this secret conversation play out between the two.

Tyron leapt up and gripped Chance around the throat, hoisted him up and slammed his head against the wall. 'You stay away from Lawlie.' He breathed so close to his face that Chance could almost taste his disdain.

Chance unlocked Tyron's hands from his throat and shoved him in the chest.

Tyron continued, 'She is too different from you, she is probably the only one who isn't doing anything to better herself, she just wants to save her zone, all the zones and you want neither of those things.'

Tyron and Chance were silent, daring each other to answer, as if waiting for the other to give away some important piece of information for the other to use.

Chance sighed, knowing he would never reason with Tyron. They were literally from two different zones. 'Believe what you will, but we still need to work out how to get out of here before they kill us both.'

Tyron stopped kicking at the cell floor and nodded. 'You're right. Now listen, rich boy, here's what we're going to do.'

Chance looked up as Tyron continued, 'We need to overpower whoever comes in to get you, Chance. If there are two Free Dayers, we will be alright. If there are five, we might have a problem.'

Chance interrupted, 'I can pretend I'm injured and you can act completely uninterested and uncaring. Not an act completely for you.' Tyron rolled his eyes as Chance continued. 'Once the

Free Dayers are inside the cell, we jump them, smash them to the ground and make our escape, easy right?' Tyron nodded in agreement, 'Alright let's do this!'

I stood nervously watching them on the screen wanting to help, but knowing there was no way I could.

I wondered if once they were free, they had a plan besides getting to the Citadel and finding me before I'm sacrificed at the Burning of the Light Ceremony. Chance knew the area well and had accompanied his father there for many years and had seen many sacrifices in his time. I didn't know if Tyron had ever been, but just like me, he wouldn't stop until he found it.

It didn't take long for the Free Dayers to come and collect Chance. Instead of two, it was three and I knew Tyron recognised them. Two of them they could take, but one, one huge guy would be a problem.

'Well if it isn't Tyron, the traitor,' the giant spoke as I watched him, his shaved head and broad shoulders leading the way. He was wearing a ripped blue singlet with faded army greens, and he led the other two scrawny guards behind him as they entered the cell block. The two skinny boys looked like new recruits, younger boys with freckles and longish brown hair, I didn't recognise them, but I assumed Tyron had known the big one for too many years.

'Ah, big boy! You've finally snuck your way up to the top of Tash's ladder. I suppose Tash really didn't have many to choose from if you were next in line.' Tyron knew how to get this enormous guy riled up and knew his temper would get the better of him, allowing for the perfect distraction.

The giant spoke, 'I just want you dead. I would have turned you in to the Prestige years ago if it wasn't for Tash. You see me and her, we've been together, behind your loser back and you didn't even know.'

Tyron laughed. 'Oh I know all about you, how you write her poetry and spell almost all the words incorrectly, even her name, and your embarrassing love notes with letters written backwards. Pathetic!' Was Tyron bluffing?

If he was it didn't matter, the gigantor was fuming! And that was it, that was the button Tyron needed to push. The big guy flew at Tyron and seized him around the throat. That was Chance's cue to moan about his sore leg and as the other two dimwits tried to lift him, Chance pulled a broken wooden leg from the smashed chair out from behind his back and smacked them both, baseball style in their shins, both dropping to the ground in excruciating pain.

In the midst of strangling Tyron, the gigantor spun around to see what the commotion was, allowing Tyron enough time to knee him in the stomach, push his body backwards towards Chance and give him a clear shot at another home run. SMACK! The giant dropped to ground like a dead weight.

'Yah!' I yelled, watching them overpower the three Free Dayers.

'Not bad, hey,' Chance said smiling and swinging the broken chair leg around in the air.

'Next time, get the big one before he half strangles me to death. Now get your stuff, we gotta go.'

Chance stopped swinging the chair leg appearing suddenly nervous. 'But, how are we going to do this? You will need to swap me for her and escape unharmed.' Tyron was surprised at Chance's reaction as he picked up the giant's evaporation gun ready for service.

'I'll take you in, as my prisoner, we'll do the swap and I'll collect Lawlie, and that's it.'

'But I don't want to stay there anymore.' Chance's voice was low and sad as Tyron glanced over at him nervously.

'What do you mean? You have to, you're the trade, and this is your home, your family.'

Chance was staring back at him. 'I don't know who my family is, but I can't stay with him any longer and pretend he is my father.' Tyron sighed heavily, trying to deal with Chance, who was appearing to have some sort of meltdown.

'Well, what do you want? Where will you go?' Even though Tyron technically still hated him, he was beginning to feel sorry for the guy, after all he had no one really and his fake father was a snake.

'I'll go with you. You and Lawlie, please, I have mirc, we can run.' Tyron rolled his eyes, sometimes he hated caring about people.

'Okay, but only for a bit. We'll get you out, but then you're on your own and you have to give us some mirc.' Chance smiled, hopeful and grateful that he would finally be rid of Sceptre. And although Sceptre would probably send Captors to find him, he didn't care.

And with that, they locked the cell from the outside and left the three unconscious Free Dayers in a heap on the ground.

CHAPTER 28

I COULD HEAR SKULL returning as the lock clicked twice. This time, I switched off the screen and resumed my position, exactly where he had left me.

'Okay, you, let's go. It's time for you to become the sacrifice. Here, put these on.' He threw me a long gold dress and a flowered headpiece. I recognised the attire from the numerous sacrifices before me. This was it, this was really happening.

He untied my hands temporarily so I could put the clothes over my own, then he quickly re-tied them behind my back, 'Just so you don't try anything.'

'You mean like this!' I shot back, kicking him as hard as I could in his shin. He jumped back in pain.

'Ahhh not again. You–you–' Then he quickly composed himself and grinned. 'You will be gone soon. Now let's go.'

He marched me out the door and down a long corridor. I wasn't scared. I was quickly becoming more and more angry.

As we exited the palace, I was shoved into a large truck. It smelt like Skull and I almost choked on the stench.

'Gross, don't you wash? Surely you have enough water, I mean, you steal everything.'

He laughed. 'Mind your own business, little lady.' I rolled my eyes.

'Enough with the 'little lady' stuff. I've certainly caused you enough problems for one day.'

He drove on in silence, we were heading for the Citadel and I was pretty sure I didn't have that long to live.

On arrival, some guards let us in and I could already see the stage and a huge Double U screen on display for all to see. Skull unloaded me from the truck, pushing me out roughly, I assumed in retaliation for my stinky comments earlier.

I could see Sceptre already on stage, he had begun his address to Virozone.

'Good evening, Virozone we are here tonight at the Citadel to celebrate the Burning of the Light Ceremony. Tonight you are very fortunate, as we have a sacrifice that is both fearless and brave, a trespasser in the Prestige Zone, she who took an I.D. Brace. She who conspired with the Free Day Army and she who attempted to overthrow me in my own realm.' Sceptre's voice was loud and bold as it always was when it was Double U screened to the zones. The live streaming of the Burning of the Light Ceremony was projected into each and every household in all zones for everyone to watch. The difference was, most PreZoners embraced the ceremony, organised dinner parties and relished the tradition. While the sacrifice was always from one of the poorer zones and those zones looked at it as a tragedy as they sat in their homes waiting for one of their own to be evaporated. Sceptre continued to address the crowd and the viewers at home as I watched, held tightly in Skull's grip.

Sceptre continued, 'So let me tell you a story, my friends, and those who are not my friends. This particular AirZoner dared to challenge my authority, and in an attempt to do so, dared to confront my son and let those Free Dayers kidnap him.'

Sceptre was sitting in front of the glass chamber where all sacrifices are laid. He was wearing his finest jewels and newly polished crown, complete with golden robe and staff. This was no different to any other Burning of the Light Ceremony, he would go into some detail about the sacrifice and how she or he had wronged the Prestige in one way or another and then they would be evaporated. The Prestige would cheer and celebrate through the night and other zones would be secretly thankful it wasn't one of their family members.

'This AirZoner was busy interrogating my son so that members of the Free Day movement could break into my palace and kidnap him. The same Free Dayers who demand I abdicate the throne to get my son back. Now, you all know very well that I do not give in to ransom demands, specifically ones that involve me giving up my leadership. So here I am, ready to sacrifice this AirZoner, waiting for the safe return of my son, Chance. The Free Day Army leader Natasha De'Lane, wants my leadership for my son. Of course I fear she underestimates her partner, Tyron Silver.' Sceptre roared laughing. So Sceptre's plan was to trade me for Chance, not Chance for Virozone. My life depended on Tash growing a heart or Tyron convincing her to grow one, both unlikely.

Sceptre continued to explain the series of events that had recently taken place over the past twenty-four hours. He was daring Tash to appear with his son and trade. He hoped his plan would work. But Tash would not trade Chance for an unknown AirZoner. Sceptre would never normally go into so much detail, my sacrifice must be a big deal.

Sceptre continued.

'So I know you are watching, Natasha, you have exactly five minutes to bring my son here and trade him for the sacrifice tonight. Yes, I, Sceptre, will trade tonight's sacrifice for the return of my son. The time starts now. Skull, bring out the sacrifice.'

* * *

I was being pushed by Skull's skinny fingers across the stage and I promised myself I wouldn't cry, no, instead I would channel my anger and hope that I could figure out how to get out of his wiry grip. It couldn't be that hard. I had to be stronger than him.

He had my arms behind my back, with his left hand, and in his right hand I saw the evaporation gun. I realised that it was pointless trying to overpower him, he would just evaporate me anyway.

He whispered in my ear as he bumped me across the stage. 'Where are your little boyfriends now, girly?' I wasn't about to settle for defeat yet. Skull had organised this whole thing, and put me in a position where it was almost impossible for me to escape. But anything was possible and I would have to pull out every last bit of energy I had to get off this stage and not become the next sacrifice.

CHAPTER 29

Sceptre's voice roared loud and clear, 'Virozone, I present to you, your sacrifice.' Skull pushed me out to the front of the stage for all to see as I kicked and screamed, my arms still held behind my back. I wondered if Cobin was watching me from Jewel's house. Would he recognise me? My normal clothes had been covered with the long golden dress and flower headpiece. Most sacrifices cried and pleaded for their lives, many wept and even tried to bribe their way out, with what little mirc they had. But not me. Anyone who knew me knew I wouldn't do that.

Instead I was yelling as loud as I could, 'How dare you do this? I will NOT be the sacrifice. How long can this go on for? YOU, you Prestige should be ashamed of yourselves. We are people too, and YOU, you use us for your own entertainment.' I continued to scream, kicking the outside of the chamber with my feet trying to block my entry, but Skull held me tight, his little protruding teeth poking out as he grinned in satisfaction. He opened the chamber door.

'TYRON!' I began to scream as Skull threw me into the glass chamber and cuffed my arms and ankles to the top of the masonite slab. He whispered in my ear, 'No Free Day boyfriend will save you now, little girly.' He cackled and kissed my cheek. I shuddered and swore that as soon as I was free, I would make him pay.

Sceptre resumed addressing Virozone, 'So there you have it, my friends. She shouts for her beloved Free Dayer to come and save her, but where is he? Well it looks as though there will be no trade off. Oh well, we have approximately one minute to go until evaporation. We will see if there is a dramatic entry by anyone.'

If Sceptre was worried, he did not appear so. Instead, he sat composed, as he always did, on his throne in front of the chamber in the Citadel. Skull, as usual was enjoying the drama of it all and could not wait for the evaporation to take place. But Tash on the other hand, stood by the exit of the stage and had just witnessed Sceptre's speech and she was furious.

Tash addressed Sceptre from across the stage, 'So you think that you can run this show, do you? Ha, that I will trade Chance for her? Don't you know I want her evaporated and the only person that would even contemplate saving her is locked up to rot in a cell deep underground?'

Sceptre demanded, 'Give me my son now!'

Tash unhooked her radio from her hip. 'Have you got Chance?' but there was no reply. 'I said have you got Chance? Hello, answer me?' There was no answer. She banged it against her leg. 'Stupid caveman, where is he?' She screamed into the radio a third time, 'HAVE YOU GOT CHANCE?'

Then a deep voice came through the speaker, but it wasn't the giant's, it was someone else's voice that she recognised. 'No, he hasn't got Chance, but I do and I'm trading him for the girl and then I'm coming after you.' Tash and I both knew that voice anywhere. It was Tyron, and he was angry.

'You listen here, Tyron, you're too late. Sceptre's going to evaporate her in less than one minute and she'll be gone.'

Tyron fumed. 'Not this time, Tash.' And the radio went dead. Tash threw it on the ground and ran, I knew she needed to find them. Her only bargaining chip had gone missing, and she was exposed.

I knew Chance and Tyron were on their way. I imagined them sitting in the truck and knowing exactly what it was they were going to do. Chance and Tyron could easily carry out what they had planned, but they had one minute to get in and stop the sacrifice, and they had to move fast.

I saw them running through the entrance of the Citadel as the clock and the crowd began counting down.

60

59

58

57

Once the Prestige guards saw Tyron arrive with Chance, the evaporation gun held to his back, they made way for them to enter. The Citadel was enormous. Rows and rows of tiered chairs, stacked to the roof and filled with the Prestige dressed in all colours and styles. They were yelling in excitement for the ceremony to begin. But they began to quieten down when they saw Tyron and Chance approach the stage; they parted to allow them to enter, and gasped until there was silence.

As Tyron approached the stage, I knew he could see me through the glass chamber, lying on the altar as I cried out for him, for anyone. 'I'm coming,' he mouthed as he shoved the evaporation gun into Chance's back for effect.

5

4

3

Sceptre saw them and stroked his beard in excitement. 'Well, well, what do we have here? The Free Dayer, the hero, with my son. So you did make it in time, but only just. Stop the clock Skull!'

Skull frowned, making his face even more hideous, and trudged over to the chamber and stopped the clock. He had really wanted to sacrifice me, especially in front of Tyron. But begrudgingly he did as he was told and stood to attention for more orders from Sceptre.

CHAPTER 30

THE CLOCK STOPPED WITH two seconds left. I breathed out in relief. Their plan had worked.

'Here is your son, Sceptre, now let her go. I'll do the trade,' Tyron demanded of Sceptre, as he continued to sit on his throne.

'I knew you would not disappoint me, Tyron, and that your connection with this little AirZoner was stronger than your desire to destroy me.' Sceptre was right and Tyron and Chance both knew it. It was true he wanted the Prestige evaporated and an end to all their tyranny, but not at the cost of my life.

'Let her out and I'll let him go.'

Sceptre tugged at his white beard with his stumpy hand as if considering his next move.

He addressed the crowd and what he said next, no one could have predicted. 'What do you think, Prestige? Do we let the sacrifice go for the safe return of Chance? Chance who has no desire to become leader of Virozone and lead you after my death? Chance who stands here and would make you all believe that he is this Free Dayer's prisoner? Chance who actually isn't even my son at all!' Sceptre sniggered, a somewhat evil laugh not unlike Skull's as he slowly sauntered over to Tyron and Chance. This, no one saw coming.

'Father I don't–I don't understand?' Chance stood confused as Tyron continued to hold the evaporation gun close to his back.

'You are not my son,' Sceptre spoke in almost a whisper.

Chance's eyes scanned his father's face for any sign of regret or love, yet found none. Sceptre's eyes were dead. 'So this was your plan all along? Get me here and do what? Have me killed?'

Tyron lowered the evaporation gun from Chance's back and could not believe what he was hearing. Sceptre had wanted them both there all along, to do what?

Sceptre again spoke to the crowd, 'Yes, now there will be three sacrifices screened tonight. For the first time in Prestige history the Burning of the Light Ceremony will evaporate all of you together. What do you think about that PreZoners?'

But the Prestige were silent. Their shouting and their cheering had ceased moments ago. They were happy to see other zoners evaporated, but not Chance. They loved Chance. Then someone in the crowd starting yelling.

'Let them go! Let them go!'

Then another Prestige chimed in, 'Yeah let them go, let them go!'

Eventually more and more voices joined in until almost the entire Citadel was chanting to release all three of us.

Sceptre was confused and his old face was crinkled into a frown. 'But I thought this is what you wanted?' His voice had changed and instead it was now low and sad, the authority was gone as if he was almost pleading with them to follow his lead.

Chance approached Sceptre and looked upon him with disgust. 'No Sceptre, this is what you wanted, not them, they have love and you have only hate. You're right you are not my father and it is time to tell them all the truth.'

Sceptre was speechless, his plan to impress the Prestige and sacrifice all three had not gone as he envisioned, so what was he to do now? He did not want to look like a fool in front of all the zones, but had nowhere to go. The crowd was silent.

'I think your time is over, old man,' Chance spoke calmly and clearly in front of the silent mob as he grabbed Sceptre's golden crown from his balding head. Sceptre did not flinch, but simply let his crown be plucked from his head by his seemingly more powerful son.

'And so this is how it is to end?' Sceptre asked in almost a whisper.

'Yes, it is over, you're over,' Chance stared at him, directly in the eye and refused to look away.

Sceptre stood stunned as the pack chanted Chance's name.

'Chance!'

'Chance!'

'Chance!'

Tyron ran over to the chamber and unlocked the glass door.

'You're late,' I said as Tyron undid my wrist and ankle restraints.

'Am I ever!' he replied as he held me tightly.

The horde applauded, and I could almost see people crying with delight in their lounge rooms. It was the best Burning of the Light Ceremony they had ever seen. But then they suddenly stopped, silent.

'You didn't think I'd just give up, did you?' It was Tash, re-entering the stage, holding an evaporation gun, pointed straight at Chance. Tyron gripped me tighter as we watched in shock.

'Skull, get out here!' Tash shrieked as Skull came scampering like a little obedient dog to her side.

'Yes, dear Natasha.' He stroked her arm and she smiled smugly at Chance. She shrugged off Skull's advance impatiently.

'Looks like I win,' she addressed the entire Prestige crowd as she stood proudly with Skull by her side.

'Those two, I forgot to tell you, they're together,' I whispered to Tyron, pointing at Skull and Tash.

'I am shocked, believe me.'

Tash screamed, 'SILENCE! All of you. Now here's what is going to happen.'

She gave the evaporation gun to Skull and he kept it locked firmly on Chance's head. Sceptre had moved in next to Chance and both were now in Skull's line of fire. Tash confidently strode over to Chance and ripped the golden crown from his hands and firmly placed it on top of her own flowing red hair.

'As the new leader of Virozone I demand a permanent AIRLOCK on all zones.' The crowd gasped in shock. Permanent? All zones? No zone had ever been permanently in AIRLOCK before. This was madness.

'Unless,' she continued in her toying voice as she smirked, holding the crowd on her every word.

'Unless the rebel AirZoner is willing to give herself up as the sacrifice.'

The audience began whispering amongst themselves. Great, so I was to be evaporated after all. The masses began to boo and hiss at Tash and her decision, they wanted me to live and not die.

'OH SHUT UP, ALL OF YOU!' Tash yelled into the crowd. 'Or I'll have you all evaporated.'

They were silent.

'So, come out, come out, wherever you are?' She was taunting me to appear, after all, it was either my life or all of Virozone's, which included Cobin and Ryn. The crowd did not make a sound and waited in anticipation. Chance and Sceptre stared at Skull in disbelief as he held them prisoner with the evaporation gun.

'So, the traitor is not willing to sacrifice herself for all of Virozone, not even for her friends, not even for her best friend.'

And at that moment, the huge Double U screen shot to Cobin and Ryn, as they sat on Jewel's lounge room couch, terrified of their fate. I could see Cobin, Ryn, Jewel and Markus on the giant screen. My eyes flew from shot to shot, from Ryn's face to Cobin's as they sat, wide eyed, staring straight ahead.

'Spare!' Cobin yelled into the screen as he jumped out of his seat. But it was no use; he was in AIRLOCK, unable to leave, unable to save me. But he had promised, he had promised me he would be my spare air when I needed it. Now, when I needed him most, he could not fulfil that promise. I watched him looking around Jewel's lounge room, for something, anything he could do, but we all knew that if he went out the front door he would suffocate before he made it to the end of the street. He looked devastated.

Cobin sat back down on the couch next to Ryn, Jewel was holding onto his arm, and he was shaking. Cobin's mouth was pressed tightly shut and he was staring straight ahead. 'Who's this Tyron guy?' Ryn finally asked and Cobin shrugged.

Cobin breathed out and coughed, as if he hadn't realised he had been holding his breath. I wondered what Cobin and Ryn were thinking as they had watched Tyron approach the stage. Tyron was confident, cool and anyone could see just by looking at him that he was determined. Could Cobin see why I would call for him? Why I would call for this charismatic hero, instead of him, my best friend who had let me down. I turned away from Tyron and released myself from his embrace.

'Lawlie, you can't do this, you–' Tyron was pleading with me to stay, but deep down he knew it was useless.

I smiled a small smile, forced and nervous as I clasped Tyron's arm and lent down to pick up the evaporation gun from the ground. I clipped it to my back and grabbed Tyron by his collar and pulled him in for a hug, with his arms around me he whispered in my ear, 'Your necklace, it's more powerful than you know. Use it.'

I frowned, my necklace from Dad? I pulled away, with my eyebrows narrowed and spun around.

As I stepped out onto the stage, I pulled off the golden sacrifice dress and headpiece and tossed them on the ground. I saw my Prestige I.D. Brace and I knew it had to go, this wasn't who I was. I threw it to the ground.

I walked on, revealing my old, ripped jeans, faded t-shirt and my silver necklace, shining under the lights. No longer was I one of them in Prestige disguise. I was just me, Lawlie Pearce, from AirZone.

I saw Tash across the stage, her red hair flowing like a long mane of fire and Skull with Sceptre and Chance captive. Cobin and Ryn were still on the Double U screen staring blankly at Tyron, who watched from the side.

'WAIT!' It was Sceptre. He was staring at my necklace as I walked across the stage.

'What do you want, old man?' I asked with complete disdain. I'd had enough of him, too.

'Come closer. That–that necklace. You–' He was stuttering and making no sense, and I did not have time for this when my life was about to end. He made his way over to me slowly, Tash and Skull knowing he was no longer a threat. After all, Tash had the crown now.

Sceptre approached me. He was taller up close and not as scary as he had once appeared.

'Where did you get that necklace? With the circle and the silver feathers?'

I crossed my arms. 'My father. Unlike you, he actually cared about someone.'

'Is it really you?' Sceptre stared at me, frowning and confused.

'What? What are you saying?'

Sceptre reached out and took my necklace gently in his hand I could feel his closeness and it wasn't uncomfortable. It was strangely familiar.

Sceptre's entire body became still, frozen, except for his eyes, looking from me to the necklace and back again, but he was silent.

'What? You want to steal my necklace too, do you? Like you've stolen everything else from us? Well here you go!' And with that I ripped the necklace from my own neck and threw it in his face.

It fell to the floor and he scrambled down to retrieve it. Kneeling on the floor, turning the necklace over and over in his hands, he began to cry. He began shaking his head slowly from side to side. 'You don't know, do you? You—you have no idea?'

'I think I have a better idea than you right now, get up and leave here with some dignity at least.'

At that Sceptre smiled, and staring into my eyes he whispered, his voice barely audible as I strained to hear his old, muffled voice.

'What? What are you saying?'

'You're my daughter. You are Lawlie.'

My eyes widened as I registered what the old man was saying, was he – that he – he was my father?

My father who left? Who disappeared, who ventured from AirZone into who knows where? Could it be? No way! I snatched my necklace from his wrinkled hands as I stood still with one hand on my hip, the other gripping my necklace tight. 'I don't believe you,' I whispered it, more to myself than anyone. How could this even have been possible? That my father was Sceptre?

Sceptre stood up and faced me, I didn't want to see any resemblance in his face, but I did. We had the same eyes, the same shaped nose. 'It's true. I did leave you, I did leave your mother, but I had to. You see, they needed someone, someone had to run Virozone and there was no one else. I left you the necklace, hoping that one day, maybe, just maybe, we would find each other again.'

I stared at him, screwing up my face and completely and utterly unsure whether to believe anything he said.

Sceptre continued, 'You see, they needed a leader, they made me. If I didn't do as they said, you, your mother, Virozone, would cease to exist. I had no choice. They gave me a son, they gave me Chance and I became Sceptre, the ruler of Virozone.' I shook my head, as if trying to comprehend exactly what he was saying.

'What do you mean? Who gave you Chance? Who made you become ruler? Who are 'they'?'

At hearing his name, Chance was shaken awake and stormed over to us. 'Yeah, why don't we tell everyone *Dad*, who gave me to you?'

Sceptre looked from me to Chance and back to me. 'I can't say. I promised.'

That's it, I didn't believe him for a second. 'Don't lie to us.'

'I–I–' Sceptre stuttered, lost for words.

Before he could explain further Tash interrupted slamming the evaporation gun down on the ground.

'ENOUGH!'

She stormed over to us, pushing Sceptre back and dividing our reunion.

But Sceptre was determined, already trying to move back towards me as if he needed to see me, his daughter, up close, as if he needed to explain his reasons behind leaving, behind choosing Virozone over his family. But Tash was standing in his way.

'Where do you think you're going old man? You can stay right here while I evaporate your daughter right in front of you, in front of you all!' Tash was smiling, easily amused with what was happening and even more excited that it was being streamed live across Virozone.

'Get out of my way, Natasha. I need to speak with my daughter.' Sceptre walked directly into her line of fire and dared Tash to shoot him.

Tash screamed, 'AIRLOCK VIROZONE! Lawlie is obviously far too scared to sacrifice herself for all of you.' Tash was taunting me and using the permanent AIRLOCK as bait.

I could see Sceptre standing across from me, Tyron still holding my Prestige clothes and Ryn and Cobin's faces plastered on the Double U screen and I knew exactly what I had to do. Eyeballing Tash, our eyes angry, I stared her down and spoke, loud enough for her to hear and loud enough for all of Virozone to pay attention. 'So I'm here. What are you going to do about it?'

Tash stood, her smile twisted into a snarl as she pointed her evaporation gun directly at me and took aim. I closed my eyes, hoping that the evaporation would take me to a better place, to find my mum maybe.

But as Tash pressed her finger down, I could feel someone push me back. I opened my eyes a split second before Tash's gun evaporated Sceptre. He was evaporated into nothing.

I froze, unable to move and it took a moment to realise what had just happened. Not only had I found out my father was Sceptre, the ruler of Virozone, but he had just sacrificed himself to save me. He was gone and I was now left. I quickly unclipped my own evaporation gun from behind my back and took aim at Tash, knowing I'd have just one clean shot and just like the pinecones I'd shot with my slingshot at Death Creek, I wouldn't miss.

Shawline Publishing Group Pty Ltd

www.shawlinepublishing.com.au